Wilde Times

An Old Town Country Romance

Savannah Young

Wilde Times

A SHORT ON TIME BOOK:

Fast-paced and fun novels for readers on the go!

For more information, visit the website:
www.shortontimebooks.com

Brave the Light

NOW YOU CAN PURCHASE THE DAN PATRICK FULTON SONGS FEATURED IN THE OLD TOWN COUNTRY ROMANCE SERIES:

http://danpatrickfulton.bandcamp.com/album/brave-the-light

One

Harley

There's a collective gasp in the fitting room when Riley emerges in her wedding dress. It's a strapless Chantilly lace Vera Wang gown that fits her perfect body like a glove. Her fiancé is going to go absolutely crazy when he sees it.

"You look beautiful," Gracie sighs.

"Stunning," Patti agrees.

I shrug. "It'll do."

Riley smiles. "Coming from you, Harley. I'll take that as a compliment."

And she should. She really does light up the room. I can tell she's happy. And who wouldn't be, marrying Cooper Wilde, the most eligible bachelor to ever come out of Old Town?

"Do you really think Cooper will like it?" Riley scans the three of our faces. We're an unlikely trio of bridesmaids. Gracie is dating Cooper's brother, Tucker. Patti is Riley's best friend from New York and I'm—well—I'm not sure what I am. I'm in love with Cooper's oldest brother, Jake, but Jake doesn't do relationships. He likes to keep his options open, usually spreading the legs of several different girls every week.

"I think you have a winner," Patti assures her.

Riley glances at herself in the mirror. "I hope you're right."

Gracie places a hand on Riley's shoulder. "Cooper loves you. I'm sure he'll love anything you wear because you're the one wearing it."

I put my hand to my throat. "Please don't make me gag. We just ate lunch. If our dresses are ready, we should try them on and all stand next to you. Just to see how everything fits together."

"Great idea," Patti agrees. "I also want to see the exact color of the bridesmaids dresses again. I saw the cutest handbag in Neiman Marcus the other day, but I wasn't sure it was exactly the right shade."

Riley picked out the bridesmaid dresses several weeks ago and the shop is having them fitted for us.

"I'll ask Rosie if they're ready," Riley says.

"I can go," Gracie offers. "I don't want you to have to run all over the store in your gown."

Gracie hurries out of the dressing room and returns a few moments later with Rosie, the store manager.

"I just finished working on the bridesmaids' dresses. If you give me a minute, I'll have you try them on. I have no doubt you'll all look amazing."

Riley did a pretty good job picking out our gowns. They're a little more sophisticated and sexy than the average frou-frou thing you see most bridesmaids wear. Not that I have much experience in that area. Not only do I not have any siblings, I'm currently standing with the only female friends I've ever had.

Rosie returns carrying the three dresses and hands one to each of us.

We don't waste any time undressing and getting into our fancy garb. Of course, Patti looks fantastic. She has the body of a runway model, rail thin and legs a mile long. She would look amazing in a garbage bag.

I fill out my dress just right and imagine what I will look like when I put on some killer pumps with it. I want to look hot enough to hold Jake's attention for most of the evening.

When I look over at Gracie, I notice she's having trouble zipping up her dress. She's a tiny girl, but I have noticed she's started to put on a little bit of weight.

"I know Tucker likes to feed you," I state. "But what's going on?"

Gracie looks at us like a deer caught in headlights.

Patti's eyes narrow and I have a feeling she may be thinking the same thing I'm thinking.

Gracie gulps. "I didn't want to take anything away from Riley and Cooper's big day." Now she's blinking back tears. "You deserve to be in the spotlight, Riley."

"What's going on?" Riley looks confused.

As much as I want to interject one of my smartass remarks for some reason I stay quiet. I guess I'd rather have the words come out of Gracie's mouth.

Gracie's now biting her bottom lip. The poor girl is a ball of nerves most of the time. Tucker seems to be the only person on the planet who can calm her down.

"I'm pregnant," she admits finally. "Tucker and I are having a baby."

Riley's eyes go wide. "Oh, my God! You're pregnant!"

Gracie nods. "It obviously wasn't something we were planning, but we weren't careful either. We both really want kids so we're happy. We didn't want to announce it until after the wedding. I guess I wasn't expecting not to fit into my dress this soon."

"How far along are you?" Riley asks.

"Almost four months."

Riley's eyes go wide again and we all reflexively look down at Gracie's abdomen. She's gained a bit of weight, but she definitely hasn't popped yet. But she may in a few more weeks when the wedding takes place. She has such a small frame she can't hide much.

"Are you and Tucker going to get married?" Riley asks.

Gracie nods. "We will. After your wedding. We're just going to go downtown to the courthouse. Something like that."

Riley's already shaking her head before Gracie stops talking. "You can't just go to the courthouse. Not when Cooper and I are having a huge wedding. It's not fair."

Gracie looks like she's blinking back tears again. She's such a sensitive person. It doesn't take much to upset her. I should know. I'm a master at upsetting people and she's one of the easiest people to upset.

"I don't have any family. Just my brother, Shane. And you're my only friends. It doesn't make sense to have a big wedding. There's no one to invite."

Now Riley looks like she's going to start crying.

I suddenly feel like there's way too much estrogen in this small room. I'm going to need to escape soon.

"You and Tucker should get married with us. We can have a double wedding."

Gracie shakes her head. "No, this is your special day. I don't want to ruin it."

"You wouldn't be ruining it. You'd be making it even more special."

"What will Cooper say?"

Riley laughs. "Don't the Wilde brothers do whatever makes their women happy?"

I know she didn't mean it, but I feel like Riley's just slapped me in the face. "Not all of the Wilde brothers," I practically spit.

I can see Riley's face grow red. "Well Cooper and Tucker would do anything to make their women happy."

"And Hunter, too," Patti adds. "He did just move across the country to be with America's Sweetheart, Katie Lawrence."

The youngest Wilde brother is a cop, but he gave up his dream job in New Jersey to move to LA to be with the two time Academy Award winner, Katie Lawrence.

"Just say it," I practically scream. "The Wilde brothers are national treasures and you're all lucky bitches because you've got knights in shining armor. Except for that one brother, Jake. He's a real dog. God help any girl who falls for that player, because he won't do anything for her. He won't make any promises. He won't even keep his dick in his pants."

I can't get out of the dressing room fast enough. I'm running, but I'm not even sure where I'm running to. I just want to get away from everyone. I want to get as far away from my life as possible, but I could never run far enough.

For as long as I can remember my dream was to be with Jake Wilde. With his boyish good looks and his killer smile he could charm his way into any girl's heart. And he charmed his way into mine at an early age. Of course he didn't think twice about me when we were growing up. And why should he? He was the most popular guy in high school, the star quarterback, and I was the little girl who lived next door.

I couldn't wait to grow up and be the kind of girl that Jake Wilde would finally give a second look.

Too bad now that I am that girl, I'm not the only one he gives second looks to, or tumbles in the back room on a daily basis.

I only have about two minutes of peace before Riley, Gracie and Patti find me sitting in my Mustang. But at least I'm not crying. I can still maintain my hard-as-nails image for a little while longer, even if I'm falling apart inside.

"Are you okay?" Riley sounds overly concerned, which is typical. She cares a lot more about other people than I tend to.

I nod.

"You don't look okay." I'm surprised Gracie is so forthright, but the two of us have become close working together on a daily basis. We're an unlikely pair. Other than both being blondes, and being in love with Wilde boys, we have little else in common.

Gracie had a really hard life. She was a victim of abuse and violence at a very young age. I'm an only child from a well-off family who was spoiled beyond belief by both of my parents.

Gracie is kind and gentle and sweet as pie. She's as close to an angel as you can have on Earth.

And I'm none of those things.

Maybe another reason it's so difficult for me to come to terms with not getting Jake is because I'm so used to getting everything I want when I want it. I'm not the kind of person who takes no for an answer very easily.

"I'll be fine," I assure them.

When Patti looks at me she has fire in her eyes. "You can do a lot better than that dick, Jake Wilde." She looks at Riley and then at Gracie. "No offense to the other Wilde brothers, who are both great guys by the way." Then she looks back at me. "You're young and hot as hell. I see the way guys look at you. They salivate like puppy dogs. You could have your pick of the litter. Don't settle for a dog with fleas."

I heave a sigh. If she only knew how many times I tried to tell myself the same thing. How many times I wished I could look at another guy—any guy—and have even a fraction of the feelings I have when I look at Jake.

"I'll take that under advisement," I tell Patti as I start my car. "I should probably get back to work. I'm sure the guys are going a little nuts without us."

"You're too good for him," Patti yells as I pull out of the driveway.

***

"That's some ring," I state loudly enough to get the woman's attention.

She flashes the huge solitaire diamond in my face. "Thanks."

Why is everyone around me suddenly getting married? It's really starting to piss me off.

The woman looks a few years older than me, maybe in her mid-twenties. She's sitting at the bar with two other young women who look like they could be her sisters. She looks vaguely familiar. We probably attended Old Town High together. I didn't exactly pay attention to the girls who were older than me. Not that I paid much attention to the girls who were in my own grade either. We were more of a mutual hate society.

Right now it's slow at Haymakers, the bar that the Wilde brothers own. It's been in their family for generations, and to this day it's the only bar in Old Town.

I'm now the only person who works here who isn't a blood relation, or soon to be related by marriage.

"Celebrating?" I ask.

She shoves the ring in my face. "I just got engaged." She is all smiles.

"Congratulations. What can I get you?"

"Is Jake around?" She scans the nearly empty bar. It's not even four in the afternoon yet. The place won't pick-up for at least another hour.

"He's in the back room." I have no idea what she wants with Jake. She doesn't look like the type who he usually hooks up with. She's much too prim and proper. She looks more like someone Cooper would go for.

But he's engaged too. The best ones are always taken

The woman's eyes narrow and she says, "I really wanted to share my good news with him."

It looks to me like she wants to shove the ring in his face and I have an idea why. Jake has a reputation for humping and dumping and she was probably one of his casualties. What she doesn't realize is that even if being with him meant the world to her, chances are it most likely meant nothing to him. He probably won't even remember sticking his dick in her. And I can guarantee he won't remember her name.

"He'll probably be out a little later," I say. "If you want to stick around."

The woman gives me a huge grin. "Oh, I'm going to stick around. Thanks."

"Can I get you something to drink while you're waiting?"

"We'll have three beers," the woman says. "Whatever you have on draft."

"Budweiser okay?"

The three women all nod. They don't look like heavy drinkers. I'm willing to bet they're two-drink-max kind of girls. There are three types of females who normally come into Haymakers. The regulars: most of them are older folks, my parents' age or older, who've been coming to the bar for years. They usually have a few beers while they eat lunch or dinner. Then there are the packs: groups of girls who come in the celebrate weddings or sometimes even divorces. They're usually two-drink-maxers, especially if they're with a group of girls from work. Then there are the girls who come in to get drunk and laid. They're usually in pairs, or sometimes trios. They usually drink until they get loaded enough for any guy in the bar to look good enough to screw.

After they finish their beers the women are a lot chattier than when they entered the place.

"Another round?" I ask.

The woman frowns. "I was hoping Jake would be around by now."

Me too, I think, because I can't wait to see what this woman has to say to him. I'm pretty sure that whatever it is, it'll be a show.

The woman leans down close to me and whispers, "He took my virginity."

I can't help but smile. "Join the club."

She points a swaying finger at me. "You too?"

I nod.

She gives me a puzzled look. "Were you twelve?"

"Nineteen," I admit, but I'm not sure why. I've never actually told anyone I was a virgin until I was an adult and that I lost my virginity to a man-whore who didn't even know it was my first time. But I feel insulted by her insinuations that I look like a slut.

"You were nineteen?" She sounds like she doesn't believe me.

I place my hands on my hips and stare at her. "Why is that so hard to believe?"

She opens her mouth, but no words come out. Then she stammers a few times with some, "Well, ums."

"You're kind of dressed a little provocatively," her friend says.

I lean in so the three women will hear me. "Did you see a brand new Mustang convertible in the parking lot when you came in?"

"The cherry red one?" the friend asks.

I nod.

"We saw it," the woman says.

"I work in a bar. I was able to buy that car because I dress like this. Big tits and a tight ass earn large tips."

The women are all staring at me with eyes as wide as pie plates.

"Did someone say big tits and a tight ass?" a man's voice booms.

All of us turn at the same time to see Jake Wilde approach. He's almost thirty, but he's still got the good looks and charm of the guy who everyone adored in high school. He was the star football player and the most popular guy on campus. All the guys wanted to be him and all the girls wanted to date him, including me. People at Old Town High still talk about Jake Wilde even more than ten years after he graduated. Of course I was just a kid when Jake was in high school. He treated me more like the pesky little girl next door until I finally graduated and started working at Haymakers.

After their parents died and left them the family bar, the Wilde boys voted to have Jake manage the place. He's good at getting people into Haymakers and making sure they have a good time. Unfortunately he's not quite as good at the day-to-day operations, like bookkeeping and accounting. Fortunately, Cooper is a Wall Street financial wiz and has gotten Jake out of jams on more than a few occasions.

I'd help him, if he asked, but he never has. I was a straight A student in high school and even got full scholarships to several Ivy League universities. Math was my best subject. And I'm a wiz with computers. I could easily handle the books. But the only thing Jake sees me as is a waitress and his personal plaything that he can use when he wants to scratch a certain itch. I know I shouldn't let him use me, but he's the only man I've ever loved. I've been in love with him since I was a kid, and I can't imagine ever being with anyone else. So having a piece of Jake, when he feels like screwing me, is better than having no Jake at all.

He smiles at the three women seated at the bar. The one wearing the rock on her hand just sneers in response.

Not a response Jake is used to getting. He's sexy as hell and he knows it. Girls usually throw themselves at him.

This girl, however, girl pushes the diamond ring in Jake's face. "I'm engaged."

He gives her his celebrated winning smile. "Congratulations."

She narrows her eyes at him. "Don't you remember me?"

He raises an eyebrow. "Should I?"

I want to laugh in the girl's face, but I refrain. She looks pissed. I guess she doesn't realize that Jake screws several girls a week and he's been at it for years. He doesn't even bother to remember their names.

"Merilee Winters," she states like it should mean something.

"Okay," Jake says. "Can I get you something? Your drink looks a little low."

Merilee looks incensed, like she can't believe that Jake doesn't remember her.

"We dated in high school," she says. "You told me you loved me."

Jake smirks. "If I had a dollar for every girl who I told I loved in order to get into her pants I'd be a very rich man."

Her face turns to stone. If looks could actually kill, Jake would be writhing on the floor right now, close to death.

"You stole my virginity and dumped me for a cheerleader a week later."

He nods. "That does sound like me."

Merilee's face is now red with anger. Steam would be coming out of her ears if that was humanly possible.

"You bragged to all of your friends that you couldn't wait to get inside another virgin."

Now I can feel my own face get hot. Thank goodness I never told Jake I was a virgin when we had sex for the first time. Plus now that I know what a jerk he really is, I'm so glad I never told him he's the only man I've ever been with since then. Most people think I'm a bit of a slut because of the way I dress and my attitude, but I'm kind of an old fashioned girl when it comes to love and sex.

I just picked the wrong Wilde boy to fall for.

"Look…um…" It's obvious Jake can't remember her name, even though she said it just a few seconds ago.

"Merilee," I whisper to Jake in order to remind him.

When he grins at me my heart begins to patter just a little bit faster. It always does in those rare moments when he completely turns his attention to me.

But just as quickly he turns his attention back to Merilee and her friends.

Now's the moment when Jake really turns on the charm to win back the good favor that he thinks he deserves. In his mind everyone should love him, and nearly everyone does.

He leans on his elbow and looks right into Merilee's big, blue eyes. I can see her shudder in response to his closeness. If she didn't still have feelings for him this little show of hers would have never happened.

"I'm sorry if I hurt you, Merilee. I really am. I was just a high school kid. I didn't know how to treat a lady back then."

Merilee looks like she's going to melt right off the chair. Any anger that she had towards Jake has completely evaporated now that she's under his spell.

Her two friends are also lapping up his charm like kittens. Just two more of his cheesy lines and he could probably have sex with all three of them at the same time in the back room.

But even Jake isn't that stupid. He doesn't mess with girls who are married, and he doesn't deal with girls who are engaged either.

"I'll get you ladies whatever you want and it's on the house." When he winks at Merilee she looks like she might come completely undone. I pity the poor sap who is going to marry this girl. He'll always be a poor substitute for Jake Wilde.

And there's the reason I don't date other men. Not that what Jake and I do can actually be classified as dating, but hooking up makes it sound like less than there is between us. Or at least what I hope there is between us.

But no other guy has ever even come close to being Jake.

As if my night couldn't get any worse Regina Masters comes dashing into Haymakers. She's completely out of breath, but she still looks as good as she always does. She makes me sick. I don't know why, but I immediately look over at Jake. Of course he's already eyeing her like she's the newest food that just got put out on a giant buffet table. And Jake likes to get a taste of everything on the buffet.

Regina and I could be sisters, we look so much alike. We're both well-built blondes with stunning blue eyes and don't-mess-with-me attitudes.

"Don't even think about it," I whisper to Jake as we both watch Regina hurry over to join Merilee and her friends.

The four women make their way over to one of the tables in the back of the bar.

Jake gives me a strange look. I'm not surprised. He and I have an arrangement. He screws me and everyone else he wants to whenever he wants to and I deal with it. I never say anything about him being with other girls because I know that's how he is, but I draw the line at Regina. She's my nemesis and always has been. Ever since we were in high school.

"If you're ever with that girl I'll never touch you again."

He furrows his brow. "Why?"

"Because I hate her. I always have and always will. She gets everything she wants and I don't want her to have you."

He looks at me again. This time his eyes search mine.

"I'm serious, Jake. I really do hate her."

To my complete surprise he nods. "Okay."

"Okay?" I know he just agreed, but I need to hear it again.

"Okay," he repeats.

"Good." I'm not sure I believe him, but at least he knows how I feel.

"You may not like Regina and her friends, but Tucker and Gracie haven't arrived yet, so you're stuck serving them."

"That I can handle," I say as I make my way over to the table.

As soon as Regina spots me she smiles. I know she's not smiling because she's happy to see me. She's smiling because she's thinking of all the catty remarks she wants to make and most certainly will in time.

It only takes two seconds for the first one to come out of her mouth. "Harley Davis. I can't believe you're still waiting tables at Haymakers. So much for being voted the Girl Most Likely to Succeed."

"Regina Masters. I can't believe you're still in Old Town. So much for leaving right after graduation."

She sneers at me. "You're still here too. I'm not the one who got the big fancy Ivy League scholarships like you did. I got stuck at the community college, which is a complete drag. I decided to give up on an AA degree and go for an MRS instead." Then she holds up her hand. "I'd say that plan is working out well. It only took three months to go from our first date until I got the big fancy engagement ring on my finger. In another six months I'll be married. This is my ticket out of Old Town."

I feel like I've been punched in the gut. Regina and Merilee are both engaged and I don't even have a guy who'll stop screwing other women. When I think about the strong possibility that the man I love—the man who I've always loved and always will—won't ever settle down with me, it makes my stomach knot.

I want to get married eventually, and have a family, but I can't imagine doing it with anyone else but Jake. Unfortunately I have an equally hard time imaging him down on one knee with an engagement ring in his hand proposing to me.

The last thing I want to show is any weakness in front of Regina. She'll pounce on me like a lion pounces on its prey if she sees me flinch.

"Who's the lucky guy?" I ask in a tone as condescending as I can make it without being a complete and total bitch. I'm still supposed to be waiting on them and I take my job at Haymakers seriously.

Regina waves the large diamond ring in my face again just for emphasis. "He works in the city. Pharmaceutical sales. We're already looking at houses in Bridgewater."

Bridgewater Township is a little more suburban and much more upscale than Old Town. Someone like Regina would definitely aspire to live in place that has a ritzy mall like Bridgewater does. She'll be able to spend all of her husband's big pharma dough at Bloomingdales and Macy's.

"I want a house in Bridgewater too," Merilee whines like a spoiled brat. She makes a point of flashing her sparkler at me as well.

"Aren't they lucky?" one of their friends chimes in. She heaves a sigh for emphasis. As if the be-all and end-all of life is to get married and move to Bridgewater.

"The luckiest," I reply and try not to sound as snarky as I feel. "So how did you meet Mr. Right?"

Regina fidgets uncomfortably in her seat for a second until she finally mutters, "Sidewinders."

It's a bar very similar to Haymakers in a town not that much different than Old Town. It's just a little closer to the city.

I widen my eyes in fake shock. "You're still working there?"

She glares at me. "Just for a few more months. Until we get married. Then I'll be staying at home. Taking care of house."

And probably popping out kids as quickly as she can.

I make a point of waving the order pad in my hand. I don't actually need it. I can remember anything anyone orders, but it makes customers feel better when I write their orders down. They don't seem to believe that someone who looks like me, a pretty blonde with assets in all the rights places, can possibly have a brain too. Most people don't even believe me when I tell them that I was an Honors student in high school and salutatorian of my senior class.

"I think it's time to celebrate our success stories," Regina announces. Then she glances in my direction. "A round of shots for me and my besties."

"Shots of what?" I ask.

She waves at me like I'm some kind of nuisance bug. "Something sweet and strong."

"A round of Red Headed Sluts." I snicker to myself as I head toward the bar to place the order. The Red Headed Sluts are going to knock these skinny blonde sluts on their asses. I can hardly wait to see them rolling on the floor.

Two

Jake

Those little pink cowboy boots drive me absolutely crazy. Every time Harley wears them I want to rip her clothes off and get a long look at her with nothing on but her thong, push-up bra and those sexy boots.

But who am I kidding? Harley Davis is all I ever think about—day and night. I'm addicted to her.

I've never used drugs in my life. I hardly even drink because I'm around the stuff so much. But I feel like I know what a drug addict must go through when he's anywhere near his drug of choice. It's a craving so strong, so utterly all-consuming, that it takes over your life.

Even though I know it's wrong. Even though I know I need to break the habit. I just can't give her up.

Harley deserves so much better than me. She's brilliant and beautiful. She doesn't need to be stuck in Old Town with a has-been like me. I peaked in high school and it's been downhill ever since. I'll be in Old Town the rest of my life, managing Haymakers, and that's no place for a girl like Harley Davis. She could have anything and everything she wants. She could go anywhere and do anything. She could be anything she wants to be. She deserves a guy who is on his way up. An Ivy leaguer like my brother, Cooper. Someone who's going to make something of his life.

If we ever got serious I'd be like a ball and chain tying her to Old Town. I could never live with myself if I did that to her. Not when she needs to spread those beautiful wings of hers and fly out of here.

I do my best to push her away at least a few times a day. And whenever I can swing it, I'll invite a blonde beauty to the back room for a little joy ride. I always make sure Harley is watching when I score my latest conquest. I keep hoping she'll eventually get sick of all of my philandering and take off running. It would break my heart into a million little pieces to see her go, but I know it would be the best thing for her in the end.

Most people in town, including my own brothers, think I'm a dog for screwing everyone who'll take my offer. I can accept that. And it's not like I don't enjoy the action. I just can't let Harley settle for someone like me.

Maybe one day she'll see things my way.

"Four Red Headed Sluts." Harley grins at me when she places the order.

I make of point of scanning the bar. "It's been a while since I've bedded a red head. What table?"

She rolls her eyes at me. "The shots. Jägermeister, peach-flavored schnapps, and cranberry juice."

"You used to think I was funny," I joke as I grab four shot glasses from under the counter.

"You used to be a lot funnier. I think all that sex is starting to corrode your brain."

"What sex? We haven't been together in days." I've been try-ing my best to stay out of Harley pants as much as possible. But she makes it extremely difficult between the little white lace push up top, her unbelievably tight jeans and those damn pink cowboy boots. She's got me tied around her little finger. One bat of those long lashes over her big baby blues and I'm a goner.

"Whose fault is that?" She gives me a sly little smile and my dick springs to life.

I lean close and whisper in her ear, "Maybe when Tucker and Gracie get here you can help me with something in the back room."

When she bites her bottom lip, something she knows drives me absolutely crazy, I have to put both of my hands deep in my pockets to tame the wild beast growing in my jeans.

"What exactly do you need help with?" she says seductively.

"Getting down and dirty."

She narrows her eyes at me, but I know she's thinking the same thing as I am: Where the hell are Tucker and Gracie?

As I pour the shots I keep thinking about the promise I made to her…that I wouldn't hook up with Regina Masters. I know if I did it would completely and totally break her heart.

But maybe that would be the thing that would finally get her to leave me and Old Town for good.

"Is Regina still working at Sidewinders?" I ask as casually as I can. It's a bar in a town closer to the city. It's always been popular with the bridge and tunnel crowd. Apparently it appeals to commuters who stop in for a few on their way from Manhattan into one of the Jersey suburbs.

Harley's eyes bore into me. "You promised."

"I know. I was just curious."

Her eyes are now angry slits. "Don't be."

As she places the shots on a tray and heads over to the girls' table Tucker and Gracie hurry into the bar. Gracie hasn't looked great the last few months and today is no exception. I'm sure that's why they're so late. She's been out sick a lot recently.

Not that I'd ever complain about anything Gracie did to Tucker. He'd beat the shit out of me first and ask questions later. All of the Wilde boys are tall and muscular, but Tucker is by far the most massive of the four of us. And he's highly protective of his girlfriend. If someone even looks at her the wrong way they'll suffer Tucker's wrath. He served in the Army right out of high school and was in the middle of a bombing in Iraq. He was one of the lucky guys in his unit because he's still alive to talk about it. The only thing Tucker loves besides his girlfriend is lifting weights. He's one big and scary looking guy. He's definitely not someone you want to mess with.

"Do you think there's something wrong with Gracie?" I whisper to Harley when she returns.

I'm surprised when she laughs at me. "Looks like you're officially the last to know."

"Know what?"

"You're going to be Uncle Jake."

It takes a few seconds for me to catch her drift. Gracie is pregnant. I thought all of the Wilde boys were good about using condoms.

Or maybe it wasn't an accident...

When I look at Tucker I realize he's the happiest I've seen him since he got back from the Middle East. And maybe even ever. He wasn't exactly Mr. Sunshine and Roses before his stint in the Army.

He's smiling as he talks to Gracie, and I notice that he's extra careful when he touches her. She's rounder than I've ever seen her. A small girl naturally, she looks fuller, and she's kind of glowing.

For a split second I wonder what Harley would look like pregnant, carrying my child, but I quickly try to erase the thought from my mind. As much as I'd like to be a father someday— Harley has a much brighter future ahead of her than I could ever offer her.

Harley hurries over to Gracie and whispers something in her ear. Gracie nods and they both look over at the table where Regina and her friends are sitting.

Tucker gives me a nod, his usual greeting.

"We're not very busy yet."

He eyes me. "Let me guess. You've got some business in the back room you just have to attend to."

"It's an urgent matter," I assure him.

"Right." He rolls his eyes at me. "Whatever you say."

I glance at my watch. "Should only take about ten minutes. Fifteen tops. Can you and Gracie handle that?"

Now he's looking at me like I'm stupid. "Of course we can handle it. When have we not been able to handle it?"

"Gracie is pregnant," I reply.

"News travels fast."

"Thanks for telling me."

He heaves a sigh. "We didn't want our news to overshadow Cooper and Riley's big wedding."

"How long did you think you could keep it a secret?"

"Not very long apparently."

"So are you going to make an honest woman out of her?"

Tucker grabs the collar of my shirt so fast it takes me a few seconds to realize I'm choking.

"I love Gracie," he spits. "She's my world. That's all you need to know. And if you ever say anything like that again I'll knock your teeth down your throat."

"Okay. I got it. Will you let go of me?"

He gives me another cold look before he lets go of my shirt. "Don't you have some work to do in the back room?"

I nod. As I make my way toward the back room I grab Harley's hand and pull her back there with me.

She's laughing when I close the door to the small office behind us.

"What's so funny?" I ask as I gaze deep into her beautiful blue eyes. Sometimes I feel like I'm looking into an endless sky when I peer into them.

"You grabbing me like that and pulling me back here to have your way with me. It's so alpha male of you."

I raise an eyebrow at her. "Are you complaining?"

She shakes her head. "Not one bit."

"Good." I pull her close.

When she licks her lips in anticipation I already feel like I'm going to explode. Harley knows every one of my buttons to push. She's an absolute expert at seducing me.

She's definitely my kryptonite.

The moment I put my lips to hers it's just as sweet as music. Kissing Harley is like singing a favorite song. Even if it feels familiar, you never get tired of it and you always find a way for it to feel fresh and new.

I used to live to sing. In my younger days I even had a notion that maybe one day I'd be famous. But that dream slowly faded— just like the old pair of jeans I'm wearing. With each passing year not being any closer to stardom, or even making it on to a stage other than the one in Haymakers, I came to realize that managing a bar was my fate and being a country singer was nothing more than a hobby.

Now that our youngest brother, Hunter, also our band's drummer, has moved to California, Wilde Riders is on what might be a permanent hiatus. Not that my other brothers are as enthusiastic about the band as they once were. Cooper is spending most of his time in the city with Riley and building a life there. Not that I can blame him. And Tucker has been focused on Gracie, which will probably increase even more so now that they're having a baby.

Maybe fronting a band is a young man's game, and I'm definitely not that young anymore.

"What's on your mind?" Harley whispers into my ear. Her breath makes the hairs on my neck stand at attention.

And they're definitely not the only things that are stiff right now. She can make me rock hard without much effort.

"You and your hot little body." I kiss her neck and she gives me a little shudder in response.

When she places her hand on my chest I suck in air. Her hands are like hot irons on my cold heart. She's the only thing that can ever warm it.

My biggest fear is that when she finally decides to leave me I'll never find anyone who makes me feel even half as good as she makes me feel.

God knows I've tried. I've screwed almost every female in Old Town and within a hundred mile radius.

Hell, who am I kidding? I've probably screwed most of the females in the state. Not one of them could hold a candle to Harley.

She gives me one of her sly smiles as she begins to unbutton my shirt.

"You've never been shy about taking what you want," I say.

"Neither have you," she replies as she undoes the final button then runs her hands over my bare chest underneath.

I don't work out as much as I used to when I played football, but I still try to stay in shape. Each year it gets a little bit harder to keep everything together.

Harley, on the other hand, is still very well put together. Of course, she's almost a decade younger than me. Another good reason for her to find someone other than me.

When she moves her hands to my cheeks and cups my face I can see the concern in her eyes. "Is everything okay? You seem a little distracted."

I place my hands on her hips and push her against the wall. I completely close the distance between us and press my rock hard cock against her. I want her to know how much she turns me on. "Does everything feel okay to you?" I tease.

She nods.

I don't waste any more time on my thoughts. All I want is to feel. And what I want to feel is this: Harley's lips on mine, my hands all over her body, and my dick deep inside of her.

I kiss her again, hard and hungry. There are times when I ache to be inside of her. This is no exception.

I take one more quick look at her beautiful breasts in the push up top. Not that she needs it. She's got the most perfectly hot body on the planet. I practically rip the top off her and the bra comes off just as quickly.

As I take her full breasts into my hands I notice her nipples are already erect. I play with them a little bit anyway and Harley takes in a sharp breath in response.

The office is small, so there's not a lot of room to play, but I manage to lift her hips up. As she grips my midsection with her legs I spin her around and sit her on my desk.

Luckily I was smart enough to clear all of the paperwork earlier in the day so we've got some room to get busy.

Pulling down her jeans is always a challenge because she wears them so tight they're practically painted on, but we both manage to get them off her in record time.

She's perched on my desk in just her thong and cowgirl boots and I'm so turned on I feel like I'm a bomb on the verge of detonation.

I remove a condom from the pocket of my jeans before I yank them off.

Harley's eyes move right to the large bulge in my boxer briefs.

"See something you want?" I tease.

She gives me a slow, seductive nod in response.

My underwear comes off quickly and I'm rewarded with a hungry lick of her full lips.

When I kiss her again I feel greedy and wanting. I want to possess Harley. I want to own her in every way. But I know it's impossible. She can never truly be mine.

So I take what I can get on the borrowed time we have.

When I grab her and lift her off the desk again she squeals and laughs. No one would ever accuse Harley of being carefree, but that's the way she is when we're together. Normally she's one of the hardest, most guarded people on the planet. But when it's just the two of us she lets her guard down in a way I've never seen her do with anyone else.

I place her on her feet again so that she's facing the desk. As I move in behind her I shift her hair so that I can kiss her neck and play with her earlobe. A quick shiver overtakes her body in response.

I place my hands on her flat stomach and then ease my way down to her underwear. I slide the thong down until it's close enough to the ground that she can step out of it.

Then I slide my hands back up her torso and pull her close, so the skin on her back is touching my chest.

"Can you feel how much I want you?" I whisper.

She nods. "I want you too."

I grab the condom from the desk and quickly rip open the package. Within seconds I'm sheathed and pushing myself inside of her.

She is so wet and ready for me it takes every ounce of restraint I have not to come on the spot.

Harley and I have been hooking up for well over a year, but every time we're together she excites me even more than the last time. Sex with her never gets old and definitely never gets stale.

"Put your hands on the desk," I urge her.

When she does as I instructed I'm able to push into her harder and deeper. Even though she stifles her moan it still adds fuel to my fire. I grab both of her hips and thrust into her with everything I've got.

"Oh, God," she cries then immediately puts her hand to her mouth.

The office is fairly soundproof, but I know she doesn't want everyone in the place to hear our business.

"Come with me, Baby," I whisper into her ear as I continue to recklessly pump into her.

"Yes," she replies, nearly breathless. "Go...now."

And with that declaration I continue my mission until I'm completely spent. Somehow she's managed to totally drain the life force from me using her magic.

My entire body is glistening with a thin film of sweat when I finally pull out.

When she turns around to face me Harley is absolutely glowing.

"I take it that was satisfactory," I tease.

"It was okay," she teases right back.

I give her a mock frown. "I guess I'm losing my touch."

"Maybe you'll have to try again later tonight. With a little more stamina next time."

It makes my heart ache when she says shit like that. I'm trying to stay away from her as much as I can. Maybe finally break the connection between us. And she wants more. She always wants more.

Not that I don't want more of her. She's like heroin and I'm like a junkie. But I'm trying my best to get clean and sober and quit the Harley addiction once and for all.

I know she's also offering up more so that I'll take her home tonight instead of taking home some random girl from the bar.

I head into the tiny bathroom that's connected to the office. And I do mean tiny. With the sink and toilet crammed in as tight as they are there is barely room for me to stand. I remove the condom and clean myself up as much as possible. When I reenter the office Harley is pulling on her jeans.

I pick up her bra and shirt and hand them to her. After she slips on the bra and shirt I help her button it up. It's because I still want to touch her. I still want her close to me. I don't like to admit it, but when we're apart it's like something is missing. I try desperately to fill that void with other girls, most of them blondes who look like Harley. But none of them is Harley. None of them makes me feel the way she does.

I play with the bracelet on her arm. I gave it to her for Christmas. It's the only thing I've ever given her. The only thing I've ever given any girl, other than a good time.

I've never seen her take it off of her wrist.

"We'd better get back to work," Harley suggests. There's a hint of sadness in her tone, like she'd rather just stay back here with me.

Or maybe I'm just reading too much into it. Maybe I'm the one who'd rather just blow off work and have fun with her the rest of the night.

But Harley is much too responsible to blow off work. And she likes earning money too much. And she earns a lot of it. She works double shifts nearly every day and rarely takes a day off. I'd say she easily brings in close to a thousand dollars a week in tips alone.

"You're right." I place a quick kiss on her nose and the gesture makes her smile.

"More later?" She lifts an eyebrow.

I don't reply because I don't want to commit to that. I'm supposed to be loosening the strings between us and that would not be conducive to any string loosening whatsoever.

If I'm smart I'll pick up someone else and make sure Harley sees me leave the bar with her. Now that would be more of a string loosening.

Harley doesn't say anything, but I can see the hurt in her eyes. "Back to work it is," she says as she puts her tough-girl wall back up again.

She's back to being the girl who doesn't take shit from anyone and intimidates everyone.

Haymakers has already picked up, which means we're in for a busy night. Cooper and Riley haven't been too much help lately as all of their free time has been spent on wedding planning and combining their two households into one. But Cooper always made it clear that Haymakers was not his priority. He works fulltime on Wall Street. He and Riley only come back to town for long weekends and help out when they can.

I think it may be time to start thinking about recruiting some new employees—especially if we're going to be losing Gracie once the baby arrives. I haven't asked them yet, but knowing my brother, he won't allow anyone to watch his baby but him and Gracie. I can only imagine the interrogation he'll put me through before I'm allowed anywhere near his child, and I'm a blood relative.

The night is just like any other night at Haymakers. The regulars stream in and out of the bar. Groups of guys come in to watch a game and grab a few pints. Groups of girls come in to celebrate engagements, like Merilee and her friends, and sometimes even divorces. The occasional tourist from the city will stop in for a burger and fries because they heard from somewhere that we've got the best in town. Of course they never bothered to probe any further to find out we're the only bar in town and the only place that serves pub food.

Not much has changed in the past ten years since I started working here. And I imagine things were probably not much different when my dad ran the bar and his dad before him. The place has been in our family for generations. And it looks like there will be more generations of Wilde's to take the family business when we're old—at least Tucker and Gracie will be contributing to the gene pool.

The pace at Haymakers keeps us busy and I don't have much time to scope the place for hot blondes to take home with me. I realize that as we get close to closing time I need to scan the bar for my pick of the night. The girl I'll bring back to my house for a little rock and roll.

Harley's been eyeing me the last half hour or so. There have been more nights than I'd care to admit where I got weak and brought Harley back to the house to spend the night.

Not that I don't love every minute of holding her in my arms all night and waking up next to her. I don't do that with the other girls I pick up at the bar. I don't do cuddle time with one-nighters. If I can get them out of the house before the sun rises, even better. It avoids all of the embarrassment of the next morning when I usually can't even remember their names.

I have to remind myself that I'm trying to quit Harley. That I'll eventually need to completely let her go and every night that I bring home someone other than Harley is one step closer to that goal.

Out of the corner of my eye I catch sight of a cute little blonde walking out of the ladies room. She's not as well-endowed as I normally go for, but she's hot enough for a one-night stand. I watch to see where she's headed. I don't want to go after her if she's sitting with a guy. As a bar owner that's a big no-no. I only hit on single girls when I'm at Haymakers.

I breathe a small sigh of relief when I see that she's with another girl, a rather large brunette.

"Tuck," I shout over to my brother, who's at the other end of the bar. "I'll be right back."

He gives me the stink eye in return. He knows exactly where I'm going and what I'm going to do. It's a routine he's used to. "I guess that means I get to lock up."

"If you don't mind."

"Don't take her to the back room. Gracie is resting back there. She needed to put her feet up."

I shake my head. "Nope. This one is going home with me."

"Have fun," Tucker replies with a hint of disgust in his voice. It's no secret that he's not thrilled that I'm with so many women. Neither are my other brothers, Hunter and Cooper. They're all one-woman kind of guys.

I would be too if I didn't want Harley to have so much more than me. If I didn't know deep in my heart that she deserves so much better than me.

Just as I'm about to make my way over to the pretty little blonde Harley steps up to the bar and grabs a rag to start her clean-up routine.

I feel a moment of anxiety because I know if I don't make my move soon, as the bar is clearing out, the blonde and her friend will be out the door and I'll be going home with Harley instead.

Merilee, Regina and their two friends make a point of stepping up to the bar before they finally leave for the night.

Regina says something to Harley, which I can't quite hear, but I can tell it pisses her off. She would never lose her cool with a customer, but I can read every subtle change in her body language. The muscles in her arms have tensed and I can see the smile plastered on her face is as fake as they come.

Merilee is standing in front of me, just glaring at me. She's not saying a word. She just has a look in her eyes like she wants to kill me.

I've screwed a lot of women, but rarely do they act like I've screwed *with* them. I make it pretty clear before we get busy that what we're doing is a short term endeavor. It's possible I may not have been as forthright in my younger days.

I exhale the breath I've been holding when Merilee's friends finally exit and she follows, but not without one quick death stare back at me before she's out the door.

"Do you think Merilee may have been overreacting just a bit?" I ask as Harley cleans the bar in front of me.

She raises an eyebrow. "Why the sudden remorse?"

I shrug. "We were together years ago and she still looks at me like she wants to kill me."

"Poor baby." Harley puts on a little fake frown. "Not used to women not adoring you?"

For once I'm at a loss for words. That doesn't happen very often. I'm normally a guy who has a line for everyone and a comeback for every line.

"Maybe she has a right to be pissed at me," I say finally. "Why would she carry something like that around if she didn't?"

Harley looks at me like I'm crazy. "I didn't."

I furrow my brow. "What are you talking about?"

"Nothing," she says dismissively.

I can see something is wrong. There's something she's not telling me. "Talk to me," I urge.

Harley catches my eye. "She's not the only one."

I can feel my stomach start to knot. "What are you saying?"

"I'm saying that she's not the only girl whose virginity you took."

Now my chest is starting to constrict. This can't be possible. "And how would you know that?"

"You were the first guy I was with, Jake."

I hear the words, but they don't immediately register. There is no way Harley Davis was a virgin the first time we were together. I know she's a lot younger, but she's always been so mature, especially in that area. It always seemed like she knew exactly what she was doing.

I shake my head. "No."

"No?" She sounds incredulous. Like she can't believe I just said no.

I rake my fingers through my hair. "You were already out of high school when we first hooked up."

Her hands are now firmly and defiantly planted on her hips. "So?"

I'm not sure what to say. I feel like I've been punched in the gut. I would have never been with Harley if I had known.

Would I?

I nervously bite the inside of my cheek. It's a habit I've had since I was a kid. "There's no way. You were like eighteen."

"I was nineteen, Jake."

"Exactly. How was I supposed to know you were a virgin?" I wave up and down her sexy little outfit. "When you dress like that?"

"Would it have mattered?" When her voice cracks I know I'm in trouble. Harley is starting to get emotional, and she doesn't do emotions.

"You were one of the most popular girls in high school. I'm sure there were plenty of guys who wanted to be with you."

"You're the only guy I wanted. You're the only guy I've ever wanted."

It's like she's put an arrow through my heart. I've never felt so much pain in my life. "Have you ever been with anyone other than me?"

She doesn't immediately respond.

"Have you ever been with anyone else?" I repeat.

"No," she admits.

"Why?"

She glares at me like I've just slapped her. "Do you really need to ask that question?"

I can't look at her. I just need to escape. "I've got to get out of here."

"Where are you going?"

I don't bother to reply. I just head over to the pretty little blonde's table.

Three

Harley

There's so much more I want to say to Jake, but he doesn't give me the chance. And now he's getting ready to close the deal with the last blonde in the bar.

No surprise there.

"Jake's leaving?" Gracie asks as we both watch him grab the blonde's hand and place a kiss on it.

"Do you really have to ask that question?" I know there's hurt and anger in my voice. For once I'm not trying to hide it. Not after what I just admitted to him and his disappointing reaction. I don't even know why I told him. After the Marilee incident I was so sure I'd never tell him. What's wrong with me?

"I guess we'd better get back to work," Gracie suggests. "The place isn't going to close itself."

She's right. Jake didn't even bother to close the till and deal with the cash. Guess I'll be doing his job along with mine tonight. Good thing he can trust me with the money. Since I was a kid the Wilde boys have always treated me like family and I always thought that someday I might actually be a family member.

Lately that seems like nothing more than wishful thinking on my part.

Gracie will have to pick up some of my duties, but I'm not sure it's the best idea for her to do more than she's already doing. In the last week or so Gracie's really started to show. And I get the feeling Tucker doesn't want her working that hard around the bar.

"What are you doing?" I hear Tucker ask. Gracie's got a broom out and she's sweeping under the tables.

She turns to him and smiles. She's so sweet sometimes she makes me sick. Other times I just want to stand close enough that maybe some of her sweetness will rub off on me. She could do with a little less of it and I could use just a bit. It would be a perfect trade.

"We've got to get cleaned and closed."

Tucker grabs the broom from her hand. "I can sweep. You sit at the bar and fold napkins."

"Just because I'm pregnant doesn't mean I can't work."

Tucker gives Gracie a peck on the cheek. "I know you can work. And your job right now is to sit at the bar and fold napkins."

I know I probably shouldn't get between the lovebirds, but I'm in a bad mood and I love taunting Tucker. "You know. There are women in other parts of the world who do hard labor in farm fields until they get ready to pop. And then they just let the kid slide out. Right there in the field. And they just keep right on working."

Tucker crosses his huge arms over his chest. If I didn't know him my whole life and know he's soft as a marshmallow inside I'd be scared to death of him. "And just how do you know that?"

"I read it on the internet."

He frowns. "Don't believe everything you read on the internet."

"And don't treat your girlfriend like a porcelain doll you're afraid of breaking. I'm sure she'll be just fine."

"She'll be just fine sitting down folding napkins." When he gives me his death stare I know it's time to shut my mouth.

"Tucker just wants to take care of me," Gracie whispers to me. I know she's right and maybe part of me is super jealous that I don't have someone who cares about me that way. Jake just proved that he sure as hell doesn't.

Maybe I finally have to face the fact that he probably never will.

I've never had girlfriends, even when I was a kid. I hung out with the guys and was more of a tomboy. That was before Gracie and Riley got attached to Wilde brothers and became permanent fixtures at Haymakers. The two of them have kind of become like sisters.

I watch as Jake puts his hand on the small of the blonde's back and leads her out of the bar. Before he exits he takes one final look back at me. He always does that when he leaves the bar with another blonde, just to make sure I'm watching.

It's like he wants to rub my nose in the fact that he can have any girl he wants, whenever he wants, and I'm just one of many.

I used to be more than willing to accept that. I loved Jake so much that I thought having a piece of him, even a small one, was better than having no piece at all.

But tonight it feels different. Something has changed. Maybe that fact that I told him he's the only guy I've ever been with, the only guy I'd ever wanted to be with, and it didn't seem to have an impact on him at all.

Is he really as indifferent to woman's feelings as everyone seems to think? Is he even indifferent to my feelings?

I glance down at the bracelet Jake gave me for Christmas. I haven't taken it off since he gave it to me. For some reason I thought that him giving me that bracelet made me special. That it somehow separated me from all of the other girls. Girls he's given nothing to but a good time. But maybe I'm not as special to him as I always hoped. I used to think Jake had a big heart buried deep inside. Now I'm not so sure.

Gracie and Riley have both tried to convince me that I can do better than Jake. Apparently everyone thinks he's the one Wilde brother who can't be tamed. I used to think I'd be the one he finally settled down with. Once he was done sowing his wild oats.

Now I'm not so sure.

"Are you sure you're going to be okay?"

It's an odd question coming from Tucker. He normally doesn't get involved in other people's business.

I try to put on a tough façade even though I'm dying inside. "Sure. Why would you ask me that?"

He shrugs. "Forget it."

When I touch his arm he flinches and I immediately regret the action. I'm probably lucky he didn't slug me in response. Tucker was never the same after he got back from Iraq. PTSD. He usually doesn't let anyone but Gracie close enough to touch him.

"I'm sorry," I say quickly, but make no effort to remove my hand from his arm. "Thanks for asking if I'm okay."

"My brother is a dick. You can do a lot better than that."

That's saying a lot coming from Tucker. The Wilde brothers are close and always defend each other when push comes to shove.

"Maybe I don't want to," I admit.

"You should. You're like Cooper. You're smart and you're sharp. You don't need to be stuck in Old Town for the rest of your life working at Haymakers."

"You're probably going to be working at Haymakers the rest of your life," I remind him.

He actually laughs, which is also a rare occurrence. Maybe Gracie really has changed him. Or at least brought out the best of Tucker which had been buried deep inside for way too long.

"Who is actually going to hire a broken-down war vet like me? And I don't exactly have your brains and charm. I guess I'm lucky that my parents left us a bar so I'll always have someplace to work. Not all the guys in my unit were so lucky."

I've got to give him credit for his self-awareness. His leg was so badly damaged by an IED that he'll always limp, but I think his mind and soul were scarred worse.

"He doesn't deserve your devotion." Tucker's face has turned to stone.

"Feelings aren't like a faucet. You can't just shut them off at will."

"I just don't want you to waste your life waiting for something that's probably never going to happen."

I do my best to prevent the emotions welling up inside from escaping. People think I'm a tough girl and I never want to do anything to dispel that illusion.

"I can handle the till for tonight," he says. "You can take off."

I nod. I really do want to get out of Haymakers as quickly as possible. I don't want Tucker or Gracie to see me start crying.

I just about make it into my car when the floodgates open. I sit behind my steering wheel for a few minutes and just ball. A big, ugly cry.

I can't even remember the last time I just let loose and let out all of the emotions bottled up inside.

I don't want Tucker and Gracie to see me still sitting in the parking lot. I do my best to pack my emotions back into a neat little box and store them away in the giant warehouse of my mind.

I'm excellent at compartmentalizing everything in my life. Hence the need for the giant mind warehouse.

I take in a deep, calming breath then start my engine for the short ride back home.

***

I can't help but glance at the Wilde brother's big colonial before I go inside my own. Our families have been neighbors for years, as long as I've been alive.

The long driveway to their house is dark, but one lone light illuminates the parking area in front of the house. Jake always leaves it on for Tucker and Gracie. As I look at his pickup truck parked in the driveway my stomach knots.

All I can think about is him being with that little blonde he picked up in the bar. Kissing her, caressing her, holding her. Touching her in the most intimate of ways.

Bile begins to rise in my throat and I feel like I'm going to be sick. I hurry into my house and just about make it upstairs and into my bathroom before I throw up.

***

It's impossible to sleep so I stare at the ceiling for what seems like hours thinking about Jake and the first time we were together and all the times we've been together since then. How could he not know I was a virgin? How could he not see that I've never been with anyone else? How could he not realize how I feel about him? Is he really that self-absorbed and unaware of other people's feelings?

I know every person wants to believe that he or she is a special snowflake, but we're really all just part of a gigantic human slush pile. When you love someone they're supposed to elevate you from the slush for a while, and at least to that one person, you're special.

There have been times when Jake's treated me like I was special. They usually happened when he took me back to his room. After a night of wild sex, he'd always take me into his arms and hold me tight. Some of my favorite memories are of falling asleep in his strong arms. And when we woke up the next morning, and I'd still be wrapped in his arms, I'd almost have to fight him to release his hold on me. It was like he didn't want to let me go.

I'm surprised when my phone rings. I rarely get phone calls and they're never this late at night. My breath catches when I see it's Riley.

I hope everything is okay. Riley's not the type of person to just pick up the phone to say hi. If she's phoning there's a very specific reason.

"Riley?" I say when I answer the call. "Is everything okay?"

"I was about to ask you the same thing," she replies.

I narrow my eyes. "What did you hear?"

"Cooper and I were at a benefit gala and we just got home. I checked my voice mail and there was a cryptic message from Gracie. She seems to think you're having some issues."

Issues? I try not to laugh. *I feel like my life is coming apart at the seams.* "I've had better days."

"Anything you want to talk about?" she probes.

I take in a deep breath. If I'm going to share with anyone Riley's about the closest thing I've got to a sister.

"Things with Jake are a little strained," I admit.

"I could tell you weren't yourself when we were at the bridal shop the other day. I'm really sorry if the whole wedding thing is getting to you."

"It's not your fault. And it's really not about the wedding. Or should I say weddings since Tucker and Gracie are getting married too? It's Jake. And it's me too because I'm the one who got myself into this mess."

"There are plenty of other dogs in the kennel. I know you can find one who's actually house broken."

"Dogs in the kennel? Seriously?"

She laughs. "Fish in the sea is just so clichéd. I couldn't do it."

"I admitted to Jake that he was my first."

"First what?" Riley sounds confused.

"First," I repeat. "As in I was a virgin before I had sex with Jake. He's my one and only."

There's silence at the other end of the line.

"Riley?"

"I'm here. I'm just trying to absorb what you just said. Just to be clear. Jake is the only guy you've ever had sex with."

"Yes. He's the only one."

"My mind is completely blown."

"Why does everyone have such a hard time with this? Do I come across as some kind of slut?"

Another awkward silence.

"Riley?"

"I wouldn't say slut exactly. You're more like a blonde bombshell. I always imagined guys knocking each other over to get to you."

I give a sarcastic laugh. "Hordes of guys are gathered outside right now. I'm not sure how I'll get through them all in one night."

"Sorry." Riley sounds remorseful.

I heave a sigh. "It's okay. There's not a lot I can do about the way I look. But I guess dressing the way I do adds fuel to the fire."

"More like adding a tanker of gasoline to a raging inferno."

"Seriously?"

"Put it this way. When you're finally ready to expand your horizons beyond Jake you'll have no trouble finding guys more than willing to step in and maybe even offer a real relationship."

A real relationship. I know what the words mean and I certainly have great examples around me: Riley and Cooper; Tucker and Gracie; my parents. I just haven't experienced it yet.

"I never imagined myself with anyone but Jake," I admit.

46

"You know the Wilde brothers would do anything for each other. But even Cooper isn't thrilled with the way Jake treats women, especially you, Harley."

"I'm not thrilled about it either. I guess I just put up with it because I love him."

"I know. But sometimes love isn't enough. Sorry for the cliché, but it is appropriate. And now for another cliché since I'm on a roll: you can't change a leopard's spots."

"Once a snake always a snake."

She laughs. "Once a dog always a dog."

"It's going to be really hard getting over him."

"The first one's always the toughest."

We both laugh. "Thanks, Riley."

"Anytime. We'll see you soon."

Four

Jake

I just want this girl to leave. She won't stop talking and her cackling is driving me crazy. Every time she laughs it's like she's stabbing an icepick in my head.

I thought she'd take the hint when I came back from the bathroom and was completely dressed, but she's still completely naked and hasn't even attempted to move from my bed.

There's no way in hell I'm letting her stay the night. I can barely stand being with her for another five minutes—let alone five hours until daylight.

I gather her clothes that are strewn around my bedroom and place them at the end of the bed, hoping she'll take the hint.

No such luck. She just stretches and yawns instead. "Tired?"

I shake my head. "Not really?"

"That was quite a workout."

"Maybe I should take you home now." I'm hoping the direct approach will be more effective since she can't seem to take a hint.

Her eyes go wide. "Now?"

"Now," I repeat.

She looks upset, like she might cry. The last thing I need right now are waterworks. I'm not in the mood at all.

"I'm sure you'll be more comfortable sleeping in your own bed tonight." I try to make my tone as calm as possible. Then I give her one of my winning smiles.

She heaves a small sigh, but gets out of the bed. She does have a sexy little body. Too bad it's attached to her incessant talking and that irritating cackle.

I'm thrilled that she gets dressed quickly. And it looks like she's over the emotional thing—for now anyway.

"Maybe we can do this again sometime?" She looks up at me and bats her lashes.

I shake my head. "This was only a one night thing."

Now she looks like I hit her. Great—maybe I spoke too soon about her being over the emotional thing.

"You said you liked me."

I liked you enough to sleep with you once, I want to say, but I refrain. She did just let me fuck her, and I'm not that big of a dick.

I touch her face. "I'm just not into anything serious right now. I thought I made that pretty clear at the bar, before I took you home."

She nods. Most girls I pick up are even less interested in anything serious then I am. They usually think I'm just a bartender, and a quickie in the back room or a one-night fling with a bartender is something they can brag about to their girlfriends. But every once in a while I pick up someone who thinks there's a possibility of something more.

Unfortunately tonight is one of those nights.

I push her out of the house as quietly as I can. I don't want to wake up Gracie and Tucker.

"Where do you live?" I ask, as I start my pickup.

"Green Meadows." She looks out the window instead of looking at me.

Green Meadows is a trailer park outside of town. And not a nice one either. It's a place for people who are down-and-out or down-on-their-luck. They offer weekly and monthly rentals. A lot of people go there if they can't afford the deposit for one of the few apartment buildings in Old Town.

At least now I know why she wanted to stay at my place more than she wanted to go home.

"You're quiet," she says as we make the drive out of Old Town. The road is deserted except for the occasional raccoon.

I don't bother to respond. I'm not sure what to say anyway. All I can think about is getting home and getting a shower. I can smell her cheap perfume all over me and it's kind of making me sick.

"You were Mr. Chatty when you were trying to get me into bed. Now you won't say a word to me."

"I'm not sure what you want me to say."

"It's that girl, isn't it?" It's not a question.

"What girl?" I fire back.

"The blonde waitress from the bar. I saw the way you looked at her. You couldn't keep your eyes off of her. And you stopped and looked at her before we left the bar. It was almost like you wanted her to see us leave together."

The girl is a lot smarter than I gave her credit for. "It's nothing."

"Whatever you say."

As soon as I pull into Green Meadows, the girl has the passenger door open. I barely stop the truck before she hops out.

"Have a nice life," she shouts as she slams the door behind her.

If only I knew how to make that happen without Harley in it.

When I pull into my driveway I can't help but notice that Harley's bedroom light is still on. I sit in my truck and just stare at her window.

I want so badly to have her in my arms. I'd knock on her front door right now, if her scary biker father wouldn't kill me. And if I didn't still smell like sex and cheap perfume.

I'm also not sure I can face her right now. I don't know what to say, or how to act, now that I know I'm the only guy she's ever been with.

She totally blew my mind with the revelation, and it completely threw me into a tailspin. I feel like my axis has been completely shifted.

But I have a better understanding now of why it's been so difficult for her to leave me. And I also know now more than ever that she has to go.

I'm surprised to see Tucker in the kitchen when I enter. "What are you doing up?"

He glares at me and grunts something unintelligible. I'm not sure whether I should even ask him to repeat what he said. I have a feeling I won't like it very much.

"I'm just getting a drink of water before I go to bed." I grab a glass from the cabinet and fill it with water from the refrigerator.

"Just make sure you're ready to open in the morning."

"Don't I always open?" I fire back.

He looks me up and down. "I don't like the way you're acting."

I frown. "How am I acting?"

"Weird."

"That says a lot coming from you." My brother's brain got a little fried in Iraq and it's taken a long time for him to even be somewhat normal again. Being with Gracie has helped a lot. He's actually more like a human being again.

Like me he's got a glass of water in his hands, but he hasn't taken a sip of it. "Getting some water for Gracie?"

"Some of us actually care about the women in our lives," he snaps.

"Whoa, wait a minute. Who said I didn't care about the women in my life?"

"I like how you used the plural. *Women*. Isn't that a big part of the problem? I have one woman in my life and she's the person I care about most in this world. I would never do anything to hurt her. You seem to go out of your way to hurt Harley."

As much as I don't want to hurt her I know her staying in Old Town just to be with me would hurt her even worse in the long run. Settling for me when she can have someone a lot better would also hurt her.

"She knows the drill," I fire back. It's my standard line. Women know exactly what they're getting into when they're with me. I don't lie and I don't make promises I can't keep. Although I may have a lie or two of omission when it comes to Harley Davis. She has no idea how crazy I am about her, and always have been, and probably always will be. But she's never going to find out if I can help it.

"You need to stop screwing around with her, Bro. You're going to do some serious damage to her."

52

"She's a big girl. She can handle it." Even as the words that I've uttered so many times before come out of my mouth I'm not even sure I believe them anymore. But for some reason I say them anyway.

He shakes his head. "It's your life. I just hope you know what you're doing."

Before I even have a chance to respond Tucker is already heading out of the kitchen.

Know what I'm doing? That's a laugh. I have no idea what I'm doing anymore. I try to remember the first time Harley and I were together. To see if there was any clue that she was a virgin. I remember she was wearing a little black mini skirt that was so short and so tight it could have probably doubled as a belt. She also had on a little black halter top that was so tight I could see the outline of her nipples peeking out from her bra. I already knew she was drop-dead gorgeous and it was the main reason I hired her, but the day she wore that little number I realized she was also sexy as hell. I also realized that I had to have her. I couldn't take my eyes off her all night. All I could think about was getting my hands under that little halter and then hiking that little shirt up just enough to get inside of her.

Just thinking about it now I'm already rock hard again.

I guess I just assumed that a girl who dressed like that had already been taken out for more than a few rides. I have no idea why it never occurred to me that I was her first rodeo ride.

I remember so clearly how she responded to my every touch. I had never been with a woman who seemed so in tune with her own body and with mine. It was almost like we were made for each other, we just fit together so perfectly in every way. Our lips,

53

our bodies, every touch, every kiss seemed to be perfectly synchronized.

Being with a girl for the first time is often awkward and clumsy, especially when it's her first time. But being with Harley was like being in a perfectly choreographed performance. Maybe that's why I thought she was a lot more experienced than she was.

How could I have been so wrong? And what could possibly explain how perfect we were together that very first time, and every time we've been together ever since?

Just thinking about it is making my head ache. I don't want Harley to be so perfect and perfect for me in every way. I'll want to keep her when I know I have to let her go.

Five

Harley

I'm awakened by the smell of bacon and coffee. Mom must not have gotten up early to go antiquing, which is her favorite pastime.

I throw on some yoga pants and a t-shirt before I go downstairs to see what's cooking in the kitchen.

Scrambled eggs, muffins, bacon, juice, coffee. "A special occasion?" I ask my mom when she turns around to greet me.

She gives me a warm smile, but doesn't reply. Something must be up. My mom rarely cooks, and she almost never cooks breakfast.

"Where's Dad?" I ask.

"He'll be down in a few minutes. He needed to use the bathroom."

I roll my eyes. "You're delusional if you think that's only going to take a few minutes."

My dad usually takes a stack of motorcycle magazines into the bathroom with him. I'm not sure how he sits on the toilet so long without his legs falling asleep, but somehow he manages it.

"What's cooking?" My dad asks as he waltzes into the kitchen. He's a large man, tattooed, scary looking. But he's got a heart of gold.

"How was work?" he continues as he reaches above me to grab some plates from the cupboard.

My dad absolutely hates the fact that I didn't go to college and chose to work at Haymakers instead. He barely made it through high school so college was out of the question. He really wanted his only child to be the first in the family to earn a degree.

What he always fails to mention whenever we argue about college is the fact that he probably did better in life without a college degree. He worked hard and built a successful and extremely lucrative Harley dealership.

"Work is the same as the last time you asked. Nothing has changed. Haymakers has been the same for generations."

"There's still time to sign up for the fall semester at the county college. I'll even pay for you to take a few classes."

I roll my eyes. We've had this conversation for what seems like a million times. "I'm not going to college."

My dad heaves a dramatic sigh. "Who gives up a scholarship to Columbia?"

"Me, Dad. I gave up full rides to Columbia and Harvard, remember? I also got partial scholarships to Princeton and NYU."

I see the disappointment fill my dad's eyes whenever we have this conversation.

"Have a seat," he offers.

My dad is usually a happy-go-lucky kind of guy, but this morning he seems tense. Between the look on his face and the fact that my mom is making breakfast, something unusual is going on.

My mom brings a pan filled with bacon and eggs over to the table and places food on the three plates my dad has set on the table.

He places forks and napkins next to each plate and then sits down opposite me at the small breakfast table.

A plate with muffins, butter and jelly is added to the feast before my mom takes the seat next to me.

"So what's up?" I look between my mom and dad and try to gage their reactions to my question.

They both look like cats that ate canaries.

"Your mom and I have decided to retire. We got a fantastic offer on the dealership. We've decided that we're going to take the money and travel around Europe for a few years."

I nearly choke. My mom and dad think traveling the ninety minutes into New York City is an ordeal. "What?"

"We're going to travel around Europe," my mom repeats.

"How did this come about?" I know I haven't been around much. I spend a lot of time working at Haymakers. But I feel like this has come out of left field.

"We're not getting any younger," my mom replies.

She and my dad are in their fifties, a little younger than Jake's parents were when they died. I know my parents took their deaths hard. They had been best friends for years.

"What about the house?" I manage to mumble.

"That's what we wanted to talk to you about." My dad's face is completely serious.

"Are you selling it?" I can't help the hurt in my voice.

He shakes his head. "Not if you're planning on staying here."

My heaping plate of food no longer looks appetizing. I push it away. "I wasn't planning on going anywhere."

Of course that was before my big revelation to Jake and his virtual non-response that hit me like a ton of bricks.

"The house is paid for," my dad says. "But if we sign it over to you, you'll have to pay the taxes and also pay to maintain it."

"And you'll have to stay in Old Town," my mom adds.

My head feels like it's spinning out of control. I'm not sure what to think about any of it. Staying in Old Town was much more appealing when I still thought I meant something to Jake.

"Can I have some time to think about it?" I ask.

My dad nods. "It'll be three or four weeks before all the paperwork on the dealership goes through."

I have a knot in my stomach the size of a baseball and it's tightening by the minute.

My dad pats my arm. "Whatever you decide will be fine. We just need you to make some kind of decision."

I nod.

"But please don't completely dismiss the idea of going to college," my mom says. "If we sell the house you can use some of the money to go away to school. Any place in the world. We don't want you to give up on your dreams because of your crush on that boy."

"It's not a crush. And you can say his name. You've known Jake his whole life."

"Don't get mad," my dad says.

When someone uses that as a precursor there's usually a big reason to get mad so I brace myself for the worst.

"Princeton says they'll still honor your admission for this year's class. As will NYU and Rutgers. You'll just have to pay full tuition. But we'll cover it if you decide to go."

My father looks so hopeful there's no way I can get mad at him. Even though he completely overstepped my boundaries I know he only did it because he cares about me.

"I know college was always your dream for me, Dad. I also know how important it is to you. But it's never been that important to me."

He nods, but I can see the disappointment in his eyes. Not that we haven't had this same conversation a number of times, but for some reason he keeps expecting a different outcome.

"Okay. But give it some thought. Do you really want to work at Haymakers the rest of your life?"

That's exactly what I've always wanted. For as long as I can remember I've had a vision of marrying Jake and the two of us running the bar together. But I tell my parents I'll give it some thought anyway.

***

I'm surprised when I meet Tucker and Gracie in the parking lot of Haymakers. They usually don't open the mornings after they close. Jake is usually the one to open the bar.

They both look exhausted. I have a feeling I look just as tired as they do.

"Where's Jake?" I ask as casually as I can.

Tucker unlocks the front door and we all head inside. I like Haymakers when it's quiet like this. I like Haymakers when it's noisy and filled with patrons too, but there's something special about the place this time of day, before the first of the regulars arrives for lunch. It's almost like I can feel its history. There's always a hint of pride in his voice whenever Jake talks about Haymakers. He once told me that the place has been in his family for generations and he wants to be the Wilde brother who makes sure it stays in their family for generations to come.

He's great at making people feel welcome and creating a fun-filled atmosphere that's attractive to customers. But truth be told he's not organized and he's terrible with the bookkeeping. So bad in fact that he almost lost the bar. Luckily Cooper was able to sort the finances out and save Haymakers.

I always thought that would be my contribution. Before she got sick Jake's mom ran the day-to-day operations and kept all of the books. Jake's dad would bartend and play host to all of the patrons. The arrangement worked well for his parents for years. I always imagined Jake and I playing similar roles. He could be like the face of Haymakers and I could be the supportive neck.

Tucker doesn't seem to be in a very good mood so I don't ask him again about Jake. He's too busy getting the bar ready anyway.

But I do approach Gracie, who is putting condiments on the bar for me to take to all of the tables. "What's up?"

She looks nervous, but that's not usual for her. She's one of the most anxious people I've ever met in my life. "Jake took a sick day," she whispers. "Tucker isn't very happy about it."

"I can see that." I glance over at Tucker who is banging stuff around. "Is Jake really sick?"

Jake has never been sick a day in his life. And he's never taken a day off from Haymakers, at least not since I've worked here.

Gracie shrugs. "I don't know."

Jake still hasn't hired anyone to replace Hunter when he left for California. Not that he worked very much since he became a cop. But he did fill in when needed. And Jake hasn't really been able to depend on Cooper and Riley as much since they're preoccupied with their wedding.

Without Jake here it'll be a struggle to run the place with just the three of us. Especially with Gracie not at full capacity.

I'm not sure if I should say anything to Tucker because I don't want him to bite my head off, but I know the twins, Mazzy and Suzie, have the night off from the Tawnee Mountain Resort. They'd probably be willing to help out. They worked at Haymakers before they got hired at the resort.

For no other reason than I'm tired and don't feel like completely busting my ass, I approach Tucker.

When I clear my throat he looks up at me. "What's up?"

"Jake's not coming in?"

He rolls his eyes at me. "Apparently not. I guess he has better things to do than manage his own bar."

"Mazzy and Suzie have the night off..." I don't even finish my sentence when Tucker replies.

"Call them."

The twins are young and ambitious and like making money just as much as I do. They don't hesitate to jump at the offer to work for the night.

"They're on their way," I tell Tucker as soon as I get off the phone.

"That's one problem solved." When he glares at me I know there's more on his mind.

"Whatever it is just say it," I urge.

"Whatever is going on between you and Jake is starting to interfere with Haymakers and that's not going to work."

I shake my head. "You're wrong. Jake being out today has nothing to do with me."

He narrows his eyes at me. Tucker can be a scary badass when he wants to be and he definitely wants to be right now.

He points a finger in my face. "This has everything to do with you. I don't know what happened yesterday, or what you said to him, but he's gone completely nuts."

"We went into the back room like we always do," I assure Tucker. "Nothing happened that doesn't happen on a regular basis."

His finger is still directly in my face. "Something else happened."

There's no way in hell I'm going to tell Tucker that I finally let Jake know he took my virginity. And that he's the only man I've ever been with.

The only person who needs to know that is Jake, and he acted like he didn't even care.

I shake my head. "Nothing else happened. Are you sure this doesn't have something to do with that little blonde he took home last night?"

Tucker actually laughs in my face. "She didn't even make it until morning. He kicked her to the curb hours before the sun even rose. I heard his truck start up around three and he was back by three thirty." When his gaze bores into me I feel like all the air is being sucked out of my chest. He really is one scary dude when he wants to be.

"This is about you, Harley. It's always been about you and it always will be about you. Jake's just too stupid to realize it."

And with that the conversation is over. Tucker grabs a rag from under the bar, wets it under the sink and hands it to me. "Thanks for calling the twins. Now wipe down the tables before Chuck and Nancy get here. You know they can't stand it when their table is sticky."

They are two of the regulars. Jake once told me they have been coming to Haymakers for lunch twice a week for nearly fifty years. I definitely don't want them to have a sticky table.

***

When there's a lull between the lunch and dinner crowd Gracie takes a seat at one of the empty tables near the back of the bar.

I head over and join her at the table.

"Doing okay?" I ask.

She nods. "Do you mind if I put my feet up? They're getting a little swollen."

"Is this something I have to look forward to someday?"

When she doesn't reply, but gives me a sad look instead, I add, "I mean someday if I ever find someone to have a baby with."

"You will," she assures me. "You're gorgeous."

That hasn't helped me much so far, I want to say, but just thank her instead. I have to admit that Gracie does bring out what little niceness I have inside.

"Jake can be a jerk," she whispers. He's been called a lot worse than that, but Gracie's so nice she has a difficult time even saying that about him.

"Yes he can," I agree.

"He doesn't seem to have any idea how lucky he is to have you."

I nod.

Then she leans in close and says, "I know what it's like to love someone who doesn't love you back."

My chest tightens. Is it that obvious to everyone that I love Jake and that I'm a huge fool because it's obvious that he doesn't love me back? Even naïve Gracie seems to have caught on to that pretty quickly.

"People could see that I was being abused by my ex-boyfriend," she says. "I wore the marks of his abuse on my body. People can be emotionally abused too. That's not as easy to see."

Gracie's words hit me like a blast of cold air in the face. Does she think Jake is being emotionally abusive? I've never considered his womanizing to be abusive. I've just always thought it was the way he is. It's not like he didn't make it clear from the very first time we were together that our arrangement wasn't exclusive.

"He's never lied to me," I tell her. "It's my choice to be with him even though I know he's going to be with other girls."

"That doesn't mean it's right or that it doesn't hurt."

Maybe Gracie is much less innocent than I've given her credit for. She seems to have hit the nail on the head with me and Jake.

"I can't help how I feel about him. I keep hoping one day he'll feel the same way about me."

"What if he doesn't?"

I heave a sigh. I guess I was the one who was naïve not to consider that a possibility. But it's becoming more real to me on a daily basis. "For right now I'm choosing to believe that's not an option."

"Okay." She gives me a small smile.

We sit in silence for a few moments, both lost in our own thoughts until Gracie says, "Can I ask you a question?"

"Sure."

"Riley and Cooper want to share their wedding reception with us, which is more than I ever dreamed of. We've decided to do a small civil ceremony right after Riley and Cooper's wedding at the church, but before the reception. I was wondering if you would consider being my maid of honor."

She looks so unsure of herself. Almost like she's going to cry at any moment.

Before I even have a chance to respond she says, "You don't have to. I just thought since you were already going to be in Riley's wedding, and you'd already have a dress, that you wouldn't mind."

I know it isn't funny because it looks like Gracie is going to burst into tears at any moment, but I can't help but laugh. I'm the last person on Earth anyone should want to have as a bridesmaid and now I'm being asked to be someone's maid of honor. I'd think I was in one of those practical joke videos if she didn't look so serious and utterly stressed out right now.

"I didn't mean to laugh," I say as I grab her hand. "I'm sorry."

"It's okay. I don't need to have a maid of honor."

"I would be honored to be your maid of honor," I tell her. "The reason I laughed is because I can't believe anyone would ever ask."

"Seriously?"

I nod. "Yes, seriously. I was a total bitch to you when we first met. I'm a bitch to everyone. I'm not sure why you even like me."

"Because I know you have a good heart. And I know you really care about people. Even if you are a little hard on the outside. You're like Tucker that way."

There are a lot of ways that Tucker and I are alike. We both appear to be tough as nails and guarded with armor on the outside. But we're also both soft on the inside when you really get to know us.

"You'll really be my maid of honor?"

"Of course. It's not like you have anyone else to ask anyway."

That makes her smile. "I wasn't going to say that."

"But it's true. You can't deny it. It's like winning first place in a race in which you're the only runner."

"Thank you, Harley. I really do consider you my best friend."

I stand. "I don't do female friends, but if I did, you'd be my best friend too." Then I hurry away before things with Gracie get any more sappy.

Six

Jake

I'm driving. It's what I do when I'm upset. I drive. It gives me time and space to think. Something you can definitely use when you live your whole life with your three brothers.

I'm still beating myself up for not realizing Harley was a virgin and that she's never been with anyone but me ever since. As impossible as it still seems it all makes sense.

At least I know now why she's so enthralled with me. She's has no basis for comparison. She has yet to realize that she could do better than me. Probably any guy out there would be better for her than me. Even my brothers are better than me.

Whenever I go for a long drive to clear my head I usually find myself parked outside the football field at Old Town High School. Playing on that field, being the captain of a state championship winning team, was the last time I felt really good about myself. I felt like I was on top of the world and I could achieve anything.

That was ten years ago and I've achieved nothing since. My brother, Cooper, is an Ivy League graduate. He's a hot shot on Wall Street with a beautiful fiancée who absolutely adores him. My brother, Hunter, worked his ass off to get into the police academy and became a cop. He's also dating one of the most popular actresses in Hollywood. Tucker served his country in Iraq and is a decorated veteran. He also saved the life of the woman he loves. He's a true hero in more ways than one. What did I ever do but run around on a field with a ball in my hands? I'm the manager of my family's bar. It's a great job, but it was given to me, it's not something I earned.

I'm so lost in my own thoughts that I don't see that Coach Stanley has approached my truck until he knocks on the driver's side window.

"Jake Wilde," he says as I open the window and he sticks his big head into my truck. "Long time no see."

Coach Stanley is the type of guy who never seems to age. He was in his thirties when I was in high school. Back then he looked like he had just stepped out of high school himself. Even ten years later he still has the good looks and charm of his youth. People still say that about me too, although it's getting more difficult to believe with each passing year.

"Coach. How's the team looking this year?" Even though it's summer break, Coach Stanley always runs a football camp for guys who want to play in the upcoming season.

He shrugs. "We've got a few promising prospects. Nothing like the talent when you guys were playing though."

Old Town High hasn't sent a team to the state championships since I graduated.

"Still over at Haymakers?" he asks. Coach Stanley is a very religious man. He doesn't drink and doesn't frequent the bar in town.

"I'm running the place."

"I always imagined you'd go to college. Get out of Old Town."

"I didn't exactly have the grades for that," I admit. I spent a lot more time worrying about football and cheerleaders than I did about hitting the books.

"Not married yet?" Coach has always made it clear that he doesn't condone premarital sex. He knows I'm not married, but this is his way of letting me know that I shouldn't be taking the milk for free if I'm not buying the cow.

I shake my head. "Haven't found the right girl yet."

He raises an eyebrow. "I'm sure you meet lots of great gals at the bar."

"I do."

"Don't wait too long to settle down. I married my high school sweetheart as soon as we graduated from college. Best decision I ever made. We've got two beautiful kids. My boy will be playing for me in a few years. You really want to have kids while you're still young enough to enjoy them."

I nod. "Thanks for the advice."

He pats my shoulder. "Great seeing you, Jake. Maybe when the season starts you can stop by and give the team a pep talk. I think they'd love that. You're still a celebrity here at Old Town High."

"Sure. Just let me know when."

Coach Stanley turns and heads back toward the football field, but turns back to give me a quick wave before I leave.

I know Coach Stanley is right. I never wanted to wait this long to settle down and start a family. And I never in a million years thought that one of my younger brothers would be having a kid before me.

But I know the only way I'm ever going to be able to find someone other than Harley is for Harley to get out of Old Town for good.

Before I know it I'm parked outside of Sidewinders.

This is just the place to accelerate Harley's realization process. If things go as well as I think they might she'll be packing her bags to get the hell out of Old Town in no time.

It's still fairly early so I don't expect the bar to be packed. I'm not a big drinker, but I can sure use a cold beer right now. And it's not like I can have a drink at Haymakers. I know I'm just trying to find ways to justify what I'm about to do. I'll be the first to admit all the shitty things I've done to women, but this will be by far the shittiest.

I know that once I go down this path, there's no turning back. I take a deep breath, hop out of my car and head into Sidewinders.

There's only one other patron at the bar when I take a seat.

"What can I get you?" a familiar female voice says.

When I look up I see Regina Masters staring at me. She truly is a gorgeous blonde and she has the most stunning blue eyes I've ever seen after Harley's. I can understand why Harley hates her. They're too much alike in every way. They're both the best looking girl in the room no matter where they go. They're both smart as hell. And they both say exactly what's on their minds.

"And what brings Jake Wilde to Sidewinders?" Regina is already leaning over the counter giving me a great view of her rack. And she does have what looks like nearly perfect knockers.

"Just sat down for a beer."

"Did you run out of beer at Haymakers?" she jokes.

70

"I'll take a pint of Guinness."

She gives me a sexy little smile that tells me everything I need to know. She's ready and willing whenever I'd like. "Let me get you that beer."

My eyes land on her perfect little ass that's just screaming to be grabbed in her skin tight jeans. As she's pouring my beer she takes a quick look back at me. I know it's just to make sure that she's still got my full attention.

And that she has, at least for the moment.

When she hands me the beer I notice she's not wearing her engagement ring. "Where's your diamond?" I ask.

She leans over the bar again, giving me another long look at her ample cleavage. Then she lifts a hand as if she's going to tell me a secret. "I make a lot more in tips when I leave the ring at home."

I nod. "And what does your fiancé think about that?"

"My fiancé is out of town a lot. And he doesn't see what I wear, or don't wear, to work."

"Is your fiancé out of town tonight?"

She gives me another one of her suggestive smiles. "He's out of town all week."

One night will be more than enough for what I want. "Good to know."

I take a sip of the beer.

"So what's the deal with you and Harley Davis?"

"There is no deal. I'm a free agent."

She nods. "Good to know."

"What do you like to do when your fiancé is out of town?"

She raises an eyebrow. "What did you have in mind?"

"I can think of a lot of ways to keep you entertained." I give her a charismatic grin.

She looks me up and down. "I'm sure you could."

"What time do you get off?"

"That depends on how long it takes to get back to your place. My shift is over in about thirty minutes. Just enough time to finish your beer."

"And it's about thirty minutes to my house. Can you wait that long to be entertained?"

"I've heard that you can be very entertaining so I'm sure it'll be well worth the wait."

"Good," I give her one of my winning smiles.

I wouldn't normally go after a girl who's engaged to someone else. I'm not that big of a dick, but just this once I'm willing to make an exception. Regina Masters is Harley's biggest enemy. Harley's seen me hook up with hundreds of girls, but Regina is the only one who Harley ever told me to stay away from.

As sorry as I feel for the poor sap who is going to marry Regina I have to bang her. It's the one thing that I have no doubt will finally push Harley away for good.

***

"You've got an awesome house," Regina says as she pulls a cigarette out of her purse.

We're both lying in my bed still naked and sweaty from sex.

"You can't smoke in here."

She pouts. Like that's going to impress me one bit. There's only one person on the planet who can influence me with her pout and that's the person I'm trying to push away by hooking up with Regina.

The more I get to know Regina the less I like her. I'm not going to lie and say I didn't enjoy being inside of her, but that's quickly becoming the only appealing thing about her. She's entertaining in bed—but there isn't much else to like.

On the outside, everything about her is nearly perfect.

But that's also the problem. *She's nearly perfect.* All I could think about was the all ways in which she isn't as good as Harley. Not the least of which is that Harley would never cheat on anyone she made a commitment to. Regina doesn't seem to give a shit about her fiancé at all. It seems like the only reason she wants to marry him is so she can get out of Old Town and he can buy her a house closer to the city.

She's a rotten person on the inside.

She didn't hesitate one second to spread her legs for me. And all I was offering was one quick ride. Granted I've been told that I know how to give a fantastic ride, but my rides are always one-way tickets to paradise. No return tickets allowed.

Now that I've started down this road, I have to finish to its completion. That means telling her I can't wait to see her again, even if she makes me sick, and I never want to lay eyes on her again. She needs to think things between us are more than they are so that she'll rub it in Harley's face.

I have a sick feeling in the pit of my stomach. Just imagining the look on Harley's face when she finds out I was with Regina is nearly killing me. I have no idea how I'm going to handle seeing her face when she actually hears the news.

For a split second I feel like I just may have made the worst decision in my entire life. I know when she finds out that I was with Regina she'll never want to be with me again. I also know she'll never forgive me because I told her I wouldn't. I promised her and I broke that promise.

I just broke the heart of the only girl I've ever loved.

Seven

Harley

"What do you think of this one?" Gracie asks. She holds up what is probably the thirtieth wedding dress we've looked at today. They're all starting to look the same. The obvious problem is that Gracie is pregnant and really starting to show, so it limits what she can wear, and even more limiting is what she'll be able to fit into another few weeks from now.

It's clear to me now why so many people elope. Weddings require too much shopping. And I love to shop. So that tells you something.

"I don't want to have to wear a tent." Gracie sounds like she might cry.

"Do you think there's a maternity shop that specializes in wedding gowns?"

She narrows her eyes at me. "Most people get married first and then have a baby. Maybe Tucker and I should forget about trying to have a ceremony and reception."

Now I feel bad that I'm getting frustrated with the process. I'm the maid of honor. I'm supposed to be supporting the bride no matter how irritated I may be getting. "I'm sure we can find a dress that will work."

"Do you really think so?" When Gracie's voice cracks I know I have to do something exceptional if I don't want this shopping excursion to deteriorate into a cry-fest.

"I know so," I assure her. "Let's see if we can get a salesperson to help us. You can't be the only woman who's ever been in this particular situation. Half the movie stars in Hollywood seem to be getting pregnant before they get married."

"Okay," she agrees.

Fortunately when we're finally able to find someone to help us she has a lot of ideas for dresses that might work for Gracie. Apparently there really are lines of maternity wedding dresses.

And Gracie tries on all twelve of the ones in the shop.

When we finally have the field narrowed down to three possible dresses she can't seem to make the final decision.

I take a quick glance at the clock on my smartphone and notice we've been at this for nearly three hours. "I don't want to rush you, Gracie, but we're going to have to get to Haymakers soon."

"I know." She turns to face me. "Will you pick the dress for me?"

I shake my head. "I'm not sure that's a good idea."

"Why?" She looks like she's on the verge of a nervous breakdown.

"It's your special day. You should pick the dress."

She's wringing her hands. She does that a lot when she's anxious.

"Tell me what's really going on."

She glances at the salesperson, who is now helping another customer, then back over at me. Then she whispers so quietly I can barely hear her, "These dresses are really expensive."

I smile. "Wedding dresses usually are. But it's hopefully a once-in-a-lifetime expense."

She nods, but still looks so unsure.

"You've been saving your tip money, haven't you?" I ask.

She makes good money working at Haymakers and knowing Tucker as well as I do he probably doesn't ask her to pay for anything. I would find it hard to believe that she doesn't have enough money to easily afford any of these dresses.

"Tucker gave me money for a dress," she whispers.

"How much?"

"A thousand dollars."

I look at the price tags on the dresses. Not one of them is even close to that.

"You have plenty of money," I tell her.

"I'm afraid to spend that much."

"It's okay," I assure her. "Tucker wouldn't have given it to you if he didn't want you to spend it."

"Are you sure?" She looks like she might burst into tears at any moment. I don't know a lot of the details of what she went through with her crazy abusive ex, but he did try to kill both her and Tucker, so I know it wasn't good. But it's times like these that I'm really aware of how damaged she was by everything that happened to her.

"I'm sure. Pick the dress you like the best. It'll be okay."

She looks very carefully at each of the three dresses again before she finally makes a decision. "I want this one."

She holds up the simple, but elegant gown.

"It's beautiful," I tell her. I do think the dress is lovely, but I want to get the hell out of the store even more.

"Thanks for being here with me," she says as we take the dress to the salesperson.

"I think you made a good choice."

She gives me a big grin in response.

"And we'll have just enough time to get you back home so you can get changed and ready for work."

***

Before Gracie has a chance to open the front door, it flies opens. I take a few steps back and to my surprise out walks Jake with Regina Masters.

What the hell is he doing with Regina Masters?

Not that it isn't completely obvious what he was doing with her. He looks freshly showered and she looks freshly fucked.

He knows how much I hate her. I've told him more than a few times. I even asked him never to hook up with her and he promised me he wouldn't. I guess that promise, like everything else to do with me, didn't mean very much to him.

When Regina sees me she gives me a catty little grin. It was no secret when we were in school that I had a thing for Jake Wilde.

"I had a great time, Jake." Regina makes a point of smiling back at me before she plants a kiss on his lips. "And I'll definitely take you up on your offer for a little extra-marital entertainment whenever I want."

Seriously? Jake never does repeat performances. Not with anyone but me.

How could he say that? How could he say that to her of all people?

I feel like I'm going to throw up.

"You're not here for Jake, are you?" Regina is now eyeing me. "I think he's had his fill for a while."

78

She obviously doesn't know Jake as well as she thinks. He never has enough.

I stare at her naked finger. Her diamond engagement ring is nowhere to be seen. "What does your fiancé have to say about you spending the night with Jake?"

She gives me a sly smile. "He's out of town at a convention. What he doesn't know won't hurt him."

She turns her attention back to Jake. "You've got my number." When she touches his arm I just want to punch her. But I think I want to hit Jake even more. I'm angry at both of them.

Before I can say anything more Regina heads toward her car.

I feel like I've been punched in the gut. He never takes anyone's number. Ever. There's no point because he knows he's never going to use it.

As soon as Regina's car is headed down the driveway, I turn to Jake.

I'm usually calm as a cucumber, but I'm so mad right now I'm actually shaking. "How could you?" is about all I can manage to get out. "With her?"

He just stares at me, expressionless. "You know the score."

That's his standard justification with every girl. She knows the score. As if he doesn't have any feelings at all. He just wants to take what he can get and it's supposed to be okay because the girl knows what she's getting into.

"Do you have any idea how much I love you Jake? Do you even have a clue? I have no idea why you keep pushing me away. But now you've finally done it. You've succeeded. Are you happy with yourself? Are you glad that I hate you?"

Now he's the one who looks like he's been punched in the gut. Good. He deserves it.

"You knew exactly what was going to happen when you screwed Regina Masters. That's why you did it, isn't it?"

"Don't give yourself so much credit, Harley. I happened to stop at Sidewinders and she was working there. She made an offer and I took her up on it. It had nothing to do with you."

Before I can stop myself I slap him across the face. I've never hit another human being in my entire life and I just hit the only man I've ever loved.

"You're an asshole. Everyone knows that. But you've never lied to me before. You knew damn well that Regina worked at Sidewinders. I don't think it's some accident that's where you ended up. You've never taken a girl's number in your life. You've never promised anyone else a repeat performance. And you just happen to promise that to her."

Jake starts to bite the sides of his mouth. It's a nervous habit he's had his entire life.

"You want me out of your life?" I spit. "Is that what this is about? Well you've finally succeeded."

I take off the bracelet that he gave me for Christmas. The one that coincidently matched the one I bought him. The one I haven't taken off since then.

I throw the only gift Jake ever gave me back in his face.

"You never loved me, did you? I guess I wanted you to love me so badly that I thought I could make it true."

"Why would you say that?"

"It doesn't matter now…"

He grabs my arm. I try to pull away, but he's got a strong hold on me. "Wait…"

"I never got a song, Jake. Every Wilde brother gave the woman he loved a song. Summer for Riley, Road Song for Gracie, and Prove for Katie."

"Since Hunter left for California Wilde Riders hasn't been much of a band."

I rip my arm from his grasp. "We've been together a lot longer than that, Jake. I just never meant anything to you. I'm glad I finally realized just how little I mean to you before it's too late."

"Too late for what?"

I don't even bother to wait for an answer. I just start running. As fast as I can. Back toward my house. I didn't even get the chance to tell him that it might not be my house much longer. Not that he'd care. I'm not sure why I still care as much as I do.

The only reason I stop running is because I realize I can't breathe. I've been running so hard and so fast my lungs feel like they're on fire. I see my favorite spot a few feet away. It's an old dead tree that fell down years ago and has turned into a fossil. I love sitting on the thing and just thinking. It's a great place to contemplate life.

All I can think about is how badly I've destroyed mine. I always thought if I loved Jake enough, he'd realize how much I loved him and how much I cared about him and he'd eventually love me back.

For supposedly being so smart I guess that was really dumb.

My cheeks are getting wet and it takes me a few moments to realize there are tears streaming down my face.

I'm crying.

Tough as nails Harley Davis is crying again. I've been doing that a lot lately. It's becoming a habit and I don't like it.

I bury my face in my hands and let go. I blubber like a baby—spit, snot and all.

Eight

Jake

I tried so hard for so long to break Harley's heart. I just didn't realize that I'd end up shattering mine in the process. I haven't been able to eat or sleep for days. When I knew Harley was part of my life my days would always brighten whenever I saw her. It's like she was able to fill in my normally dull world with all of her vivid colors. Now that she's made a point of letting me know that we are not and never will be together again my world is all gray. Completely colorless.

And it's not that Harley isn't still filled with sunshine. She just refuses to share her bright light with me like she used to. I didn't realize how much I'd miss it.

She always laughs and jokes with all of the patrons. It's one of the many reasons she makes a fortune in tips. But now she makes a point of completely turning all of her charm off whenever she steps near me. She's not just her cold and guarded self with me. She's artic frigid.

She's even being super nice to Tucker, which is not something he's used to, but he seems to be enjoying it. And he seems to be enjoying rubbing it in my face even more.

"Harley looks great today," he comments as we watch her carrying a large tray of beers over to a bowling team that stopped in after their tournament.

"Yup." I try not to show any emotion, even though I'm dying inside. There's nothing I want more than to have her naked in my arms, but I know that will never happen again.

"She looks happy. I wonder why?"

I turn to face him. "I know Gracie told you what happened. You know we're not together anymore."

"You deserve to have your ass dumped."

I nod. "I know."

"And she deserves a lot better than you."

"I know that too," I agree.

"At least we're on the same page about that."

Tucker doesn't give me a chance to say anything more. He heads over to where Gracie is standing, takes the broom that she has in her hands and starts sweeping for her.

A few minutes later I notice a tall, muscular, blond guy walk into Haymakers. He's definitely not from Old Town. Most of the guys around here wear cowboy boots and jeans. This guy is wearing a Hawaiian shirt over a rock concert t-shirt, tan cargo pants and red Converse sneakers. I feel like asking him if he made a wrong turn on his way to the beach, but I refrain.

He definitely looks out of place as he takes a seat at the bar. Before I have a chance to make my way over to him, Harley swoops in. She practically runs me over on her way to serve the guy.

"So," she says to the beach boy. "What are you having?"

When he smiles at her I feel like I want to punch him. He's got a smile so wide and teeth so white it's almost overpowering. I've never wanted someone out of my bar as badly as I want this guy gone.

When the guy looks Harley up and down and then his eyes land on her breasts it takes every ounce of restraint I have not to beat him senseless. I want to tell him to take his eyes off my girl.

The only problem is that she's not mine. And that's my fault.

Then I want to punch myself in the face for being such a fool.

I guess I never realized how hard it would be to see Harley with anyone else. Or even to see another guy show interest in her.

Maybe deep down I really did know that Harley wasn't with anyone other than me. Now that there's a real possibility she could be with another guy, I don't like it at all.

"Beer," the beach boy says. "Do you have Stella?"

Harley gives him a nod which seems a little too seductive and I feel like she's punched me right in the gut.

Most of the regulars order whatever is on tap, so we don't have a very large bottled beer selection. We do have Stella, but mainly because Cooper and Riley like it.

When Harley turns away from the beach boy and heads over to the small beer fridge, I make a point of standing right next to her. I'm a little hurt when she completely ignores me, so I grab ahold of her arm.

"Take your hand off of me," she spits, without even looking me in the eyes.

"What do you think you're doing?" I spit back.

"My job. I'm serving beer to a customer."

When she finally looks at me it's more of a glare and it cuts right through me like a knife. I realize that until this moment she's always looked at me with so much love in her eyes—and now I just see contempt—and underneath that pain. And it's all of my doing.

"You serve tables. You don't serve customers at the bar. Why are you suddenly so interested in serving this guy?"

I know exactly why she wants to serve him. I just don't want her anywhere near him.

She jerks her hand from my grip. "Why do you care? You had no trouble serving Regina even after I asked you not to."

My eyes narrow to angry slits. "Don't ever forget I'm your boss."

She actually laughs at me. "Whatever. Are you going to fire me for being too good of an employee? For serving too many people? You can't fire me just because you're jealous."

She's right, but I don't have any other way to stop her.

I watch as she stomps over to the beach boy and places his beer on the counter next to him.

"Would you like a glass with that?" She gives him a seductive smile that makes my stomach knot. "I can pour it for you if you'd like."

"Sure. Why not?"

She grabs a tall beer glass and pours the beer slowly and easily so it doesn't foam. I remember when I taught her to do that. It was right before the first time we had sex. It wasn't very long after she started working at Haymakers. I knew from the moment I hired her that I wanted her—in every way that a man can want a woman. She definitely wasn't that little girl from next door anymore. She was a very sexy young woman.

How could I possibly know she was a virgin? And why didn't she tell me until now?

I watch as she places her elbows on the bar in front of the beach boy and rests her head on her fists. The guy is just lapping up the attention.

I've put Haymakers ahead of everything else in my life and I respect my customers, but I want nothing more right now than for this beach boy to leave.

"Are you traveling through town?" Harley asks.

He shakes his head, then swallows his first sip of beer before he replies. "Just moved here. From the shore."

"I would have never guessed." Harley is one of the most brilliant people I've ever met in my life. She could give Cooper a run for his money and he's an Ivy League graduate. But with this guy she's putting on a real coy act.

"Max Elliot." When the guy puts out a hand for her to shake I want to rip his arm right out of the socket.

I know I should probably make myself busy doing something else, but it's kind of like when you drive by a car accident. You know you shouldn't stop and look but you just can't help yourself.

When she takes his hand she holds it way too long for my taste and then she bats her beautiful blue eyes at him before she says, "I'm Harley."

I know if he's anything like me he'll do anything those gorgeous blue eyes ask him to.

He laughs. "Like the motorcycle?"

She nods. "My dad owns the local Harley dealership. For a few more weeks anyway."

It takes a moment for those words to register. What does she mean for a few more weeks? Her parents have owned the Harley dealership for as long as I've been alive.

"Well you're much prettier than a motorcycle." When Max gives her another one of his gigantic smiles I want to punch it right off of his pretty beach boy face. I've had about all of this guy that I can take.

I step up to Harley and say, "I think some of your tables need attending to."

The contempt in her eyes cuts me like a razor, but I try my best not to react.

"Yes, Boss," she says with complete and utter disgust in her voice.

Then she turns back to Max and says, "Maybe we can continue our conversation after I get off work."

Max nods and all I can think about is showing him to the door. My mind is filled with thoughts of the two of them together. His hand on Harley, his lips touching hers. I want to scream that she's mine, but I know it's not true.

Not anymore anyway. I made sure of that.

And it was probably the biggest mistake of my life.

Harley does what I asked and waits on all of her tables. We're not that busy yet so it only takes a few minutes for her to make the rounds.

"Satisfied?" she asks as she marches by me.

"Very," I snap back.

"Good." She twists back to glare at me. "I wouldn't want to make my boss mad."

"Well you're doing a really good job of that."

"Why? I'm doing my job. Isn't that what you want? Isn't that what you pay me for?"

I'm so angry I could spit nails, but I know most of the anger is at myself.

As Max takes the last sip of his beer Harley swoops in again before I can grab the glass.

"Refill?" She gives Max a sexy smile.

I breathe a small sigh of relief when he shakes his head. "Just the tab."

When Harley hands him the bill I notice their eyes meet for a little too long. My immediate instinct once again is to hit him. The guy is tall and well-built, but he's definitely not as muscular as me or any of my brothers. I could probably take him in a fight. Not that he looks like much of a fighter anyway. He's kind of got little a tree-hugger, hippie vibe. He probably does yoga or meditates. Maybe even both.

He hands Harley some kind of business card with the cash. "Keep the change."

The beer was five bucks and he gave her a ten. Quite a large tip for one drink. I notice Harley's eyes actually light up when she reads the business card. Her eyes haven't lit up like that around me in a while. I don't want to admit how much I miss it.

As soon as Max is out the door I snatch the business card from Harley's hand.

"What do you think you're doing?" she protests loudly.

She tries to grab the card back, but I'm a little too quick and definitely too tall for her to take it from me. I'll give it back to her as soon as I have a chance to read what it says:

Old Town Ghost Tours. Max Elliot, Paranormal Investigator.

I can't help but laugh. And not a small one either. A big, belly laugh. This guy can't be serious. Ghost tours? In Old Town? Does he actually believe that's going to be a viable business?

When I hand the card back to Harley her eyes narrow and she looks like she wants to hurt me.

"What's so funny?" she snaps. She's been snapping at me a lot and it's starting to really piss me off.

"Would you mind talking with me in a normal tone of voice?"

"Fine." Now her tone is condescending and sugary sweet. "Is this better?"

I heave a sigh. "Not really. Can't we just be normal with each other?"

She shakes her head. "You made that impossible. Now why were you laughing?"

"You're not really going to take that guy seriously, are you? A ghost hunter? I'm just glad he didn't ask for your number."

"Oh, I'm going out with him. I'm willing to bet a week's salary on that. Mark my words. He'll be back. And when he comes back he'll ask for my number."

I roll my eyes. "How can you be so sure?"

"Not everyone is like you, Jake. Some guys are interested in a little more than just fifteen minutes in the back room. He's a dinner and a movie kind of guy. The kind of guy who will give a girl a goodnight kiss and then call the next day for a second date. He's definitely not going to hump and dump."

That hurts. I realize for the first time that I've never taken Harley on an actual date. We've never gone to a restaurant. Never gone to a movie. Of course we see each other at work on a daily basis. We've been in the back room hundreds of times and we've spent the night together in my bedroom a few times a week. But that's been the extent of our relationship.

Maybe I really am the dick everyone thinks I am.

"He's a guy. Maybe it'll take him a little longer to close to deal, but his goal is still the same. He wants to get in your pants."

"And what's wrong with that?" When she bats her lashes at me I feel like she's slicing right through my heart with a steel blade.

I realize I don't want anyone in those sexy jeans of hers but me.

"Don't go out with that guy," I whisper in her ear. As I take in the scent of her strawberry shampoo I'm overcome with the desire to pull her into the back room with me. I want to be inside of her. I want to make her mine again.

She pushes me away. "I'll go out with whoever I want. You don't own me, Jake."

And with that final slice through my chest she marches away.

Nine

Harley

Just as I predicted Max Elliot is back at Haymakers a few days later. He makes a point of sitting at one of the tables instead of at the bar this time. Maybe because he heard some of the conversation between me and Jake about my job being to wait tables and not serving patrons seated at the bar.

I notice right away that Jake is glaring at him. If looks could actually kill Max would already have several bullets in his back.

It hasn't gone unnoticed by me that Jake hasn't been with anyone since he hooked up with Regina. He hasn't taken any girls into the back room and he hasn't taken any girls home from the bar. It has to be some kind of record.

I intercept Gracie just as she's about to wait on Max. "Let me get this one."

She looks back and forth between me and Max as if she's trying to figure out why I'm so eager to take her table. Then realization seems to come over her face.

"Sure, no problem. I was just going to help Tucker get some ice."

As she tries to hurry away I notice that she's actually waddling. She has to be the cutest pregnant woman I've ever seen. And I'm completely jealous. Not that I have any real reason to be. Her life was utterly shattered before she met Tucker. But now she has a guy who loves her unconditionally and would go to the moon and back for her if she asked.

I want that someday. I always thought I'd have that with Jake. I'm finally over that delusion.

"Good to see you again." I give Max a big smile.

"Harley." His face lights up when he sees me.

"Was the beer that good?"

He grins. "The beer was okay, but the service was sensational. Plus this seems to be the only bar in town."

I nod. "This is a one-bar town. So why did you decide to start a ghost tour business here?"

"A lot of reasons, but the biggest reason is the new resort. All of their current activities revolve around golf in the summer and skiing in the winter. They're daytime focused. This gives the guests something to do at night. Plus I have an in with their new Activities Director."

I raise an eyebrow. The twins told me they hated the new girl who just got hired as the Activities Director. I think they called her Samantha. Of course their beef with her was that she's blonde and beautiful. She was taking all of the attention of the male staff away from them.

My stomach sinks when I consider the possibility Max and Samantha are a couple and that's why he's moved to Old Town.

"She's my sister," he says quickly, as if he's reading my thoughts. "I'm staying at her place until I get settled."

"Good to know."

"So I heard a rumor that the burgers here are delicious."

I nod. "The fries are pretty good too."

He laughs. "Already trying to upsell me. And you're smooth too. I like that."

"Stella. Burger. Fries." I narrow my eyes at him. "Something tells me you'd like a pickle too."

"Sure. I'll try the pickle too."

"So how's the ghost hunting going?" I ask.

"I've just started putting the first tour together. I'm still in the research phase."

"You've come to the right place. You are in Old Town, after all. There are plenty of historic buildings with a very high creep factor."

"History was one of my majors in college."

That piques my curiosity. Most people who leave Old Town to go to college never come back, and not many people with college degrees intentionally move to Old Town. I've been giving the idea of going away to school some thought since I ended things with Jake.

"One of your majors?"

He nods. "I liked school so much I ended up with three majors. And I stayed for a Master's degree as well."

"What did you study? I mean, besides History."

"I also got a major in Literature. And Women's Studies."

I laugh. "Why Women's Studies?"

"That one I admit was not purely academic. Imagine being the only male in a classroom with twenty to thirty women. That was the ratio in every one of my classes in Women's Studies. It beat trying to pick up girls at a frat party or the local bar on Friday nights."

"And what did you study for your Master's degree?" I probe.

"American Studies."

"What exactly do you do with a Master's degree in American Studies?"

"Run a Ghost Tour Company apparently."

I laugh. "We don't get many people in Haymakers with your level of education."

"A lot of people are surprised when I tell them I have a Master's degree. I guess I don't look scholarly enough because I don't wear little round reading glasses and a corduroy sports jacket."

"You kind of look more like a surfer than an academic."

"So you're saying you can't be smart and be a surfer?"

I shrug. "People usually don't think I'm that smart either. They judge me by how I look. But I graduated top of my class and got several scholarships to Ivy League schools."

When he looks into my eyes I can see his expression has turned serious. "I guess the obvious question is what you're doing waiting tables here in Old Town. Why aren't you at one of those Ivy League schools expanding your horizons?"

I gulp. I've started to ask myself the same question. "I don't know," I lie.

His penetrating blue eyes narrow. "Does it have anything to do with that guy?"

"What guy?" I try to sound casual even though I know exactly who he's talking about.

"The guy at the bar who is glaring at us. The one who hasn't taken his eyes off you."

When I take a quick peek back at the bar I see Jake is staring right at me, his muscular arms crossed over his chest. His face is an angry stone mask and his eyes look like they're shooting daggers at us.

I shake my head. "He's my boss. Nothing more."

Max glances over at Jake and then back at me. "You're sure about that?"

"Positive."

He gives me a sexy little grin. "Good."

"I'd better put your order in."

"Maybe when you bring me my beer and burger you can also give me your number."

"And just what do you need my number for?" I tease.

"I'd like to ask you on a date."

I grab the order pad from my back pocket, write down my cell phone number and hand it to him.

"I'll call you tonight. What time do you get off work?"

"Maybe I'll leave early tonight."

"How early is that?"

"Eight? Is that too late?"

"Considering there's only one bar in town and you work here I don't think it's smart to ask you out for a drink. But I saw a little movie theater. Want to catch a late movie?"

"It's at nine."

"Then it's a date."

When I make my way to the bar to place Max's order I give it to Tucker instead of Jake. He's still glaring at me and I don't feel like dealing with him.

But I make sure to tell Tucker loud enough for Jake to hear that I'll be leaving early because I have a date tonight.

***

I'm on the speaker phone with Mazzy and Suzie while I'm getting ready for my date with Max. I'm having a difficult time trying to decide what to wear. I'm torn between wearing something appropriate for Old Town, basically jeans and cowboy boots, or something sexy because I'm actually going on a date.

"What can you tell me about Samantha Elliot?" I ask the twins as I pull on a pair of super tight skinny jeans.

"She goes by Sam," Mazzy says.

I can't help but laugh, but I guess the twins don't get the joke. I don't hear either of them laughing. "Sam Elliott is an actor. He's an old dude."

"Never heard of him," Mazzy says.

"Neither have I," Suzie adds.

"It doesn't matter. What can you tell me about Sam?"

"Besides the fact that she's a total bitch?" Suzie says.

"And rich, apparently," Mazzy adds.

"Rich? What do you mean?"

"We heard that her uncle owns Tawnee Mountain. That's how she got the job. Apparently he's grooming her to run the place someday."

"Wow. That's something." I quickly remove the jeans and opt for the sexy black dress instead.

"Why do you care so much about Sam anyway?" Suzie asks. "You're not thinking about coming to work at the resort, are you? Jake would flip."

"Jake and I aren't seeing each other anymore."

"What!" Mazzy and Suzie scream in unison.

"What happened?" Mazzy asks.

"Tell us everything," Suzie adds.

"He did something unforgivable. He lied to me and completely betrayed me."

"That doesn't sound like Jake," Mazzy comments. "He can be a womanizing jerk. That's true. But he's not a liar."

"This was something really big," I assure them. "We're done. That's why I wanted to know about Sam. I have a date with her brother, Max."

"Sam has a brother?" Mazzy sounds surprised.

"Is he hot?" Suzie asks.

"She does have a brother. He just moved to Old Town. And he is rather hot."

"We always thought you could do better than Jake," Mazzy says.

"A lot better," Suzie adds.

"Tell us how the date goes," Mazzy requests.

"I sure will," I reply before I end the call.

***

I'm a little surprised when Max pulls up in a little red Mini Cooper convertible. It's definitely not the kind of car I'd imagine him driving and certainly provides more evidence that's he's not from around here. Guys in Old Town drive pickup trucks and most often produced by American manufacturers. You're a real rebel if you drive a pickup that's not made in the good old US of A. A Mini Cooper is definitely not something you see every day in Old Town.

I'm so nervous my stomach feels like it's filled with fluttering butterflies. I dated a few guys in high school, but nothing serious. I was too hung up on Jake my entire adolescence to even take another guy seriously enough. Of course my dad isn't helping matters any. He wants to "check the guy out" and make sure he knows there isn't going to be any "monkey business with his daughter."

My dad is one of the sweetest guys you'll ever meet, but to look at him without knowing him, he's intimidating to say the least. And I think he likes it that way.

When my dad opens the door I can see Max's eyes go wide for a split second, but he quickly recovers and has his hand out for my dad to shake. He's definitely a smooth operator.

"Mr. Davis," Max says. "Wonderful to meet you."

My dad nods and steps away from the door so Max can enter.

Max is wide-eyed again when he sees me, but I'm hoping it's for a completely different reason.

"You look amazing," he says as he gives me his huge grin.

I definitely went all out in my sexy black mini dress and black heels. The outfit is much too dressy for the theater in Old Town, but I wanted to make a statement. It'll take about five minutes from the time we arrive at the theater for news to travel back to Jake that I'm not only out with a sexy stranger, but I'm looking mighty fine.

Not that I care what Jake thinks.

Max doesn't look too shabby either. He's wearing khakis and a tight fitting polo that shows off his muscular upper body quite nicely.

"I'd also like you to meet my mom," I tell Max.

I'm thrilled that he can't keep his eyes off of me.

"Of course," he replies. "Where is she?"

"Kitchen. Baking cookies. Just in case you need a snack. She doesn't want you to go hungry."

He grins. "That's thoughtful."

I laugh. "That's my mom for you."

My parents could almost be a perfect *Leave it to Beaver*-type family if they didn't look like some weird combination of a motorcycle gang and 60s hippie throwbacks.

Max smiles when he sees my mom. She's holding a pan of baked cookies that have just come out of the oven.

"Just in time," she says as she gives Max the once-over.

I can tell by the gleam in her eyes that she definitely approves. But I think my mom would be happy with anyone I brought home who wasn't Jake Wilde.

"You have to try one while it's still warm." She pushes the pan of cookies toward Max.

"If you insist." He grabs one of the chocolate chip treats and pops it into his mouth.

"Delicious," he declares once he's chewed and swallowed.

"My mom loves to bake. I'm not much of a cookie eater so she was thrilled when she found out you were coming over."

"Let me box a few up for you," my mom says as she grabs a Tupperware container from the cupboard.

"We'd better get going," I say to Max. "We don't want to be late for the movie."

"Have her home at a decent hour," my dad says as we walk back through the living room.

"Of course, Sir," Max says politely.

"I'm an adult, Dad," I remind him.

"My house, my rules," he reminds me.

Could I be more humiliated?

"I'm so sorry about that," I say as Max opens his car door for me.

"Sorry about what?" He winks.

Once we're in the Mini I say, "My mom and dad can be a little overbearing sometimes. I am their only child."

"I can see they care about you a lot. Nothing wrong with that."

"They're just glad I'm going out with someone other than Jake," I say then immediately regret it.

"Let me guess. Jake is the guy from Haymakers."

"He owns the bar. With his brothers. So he really is my boss. But he was also my...I don't know. He really wasn't my boyfriend. It's complicated. But it really doesn't matter anymore because we broke up."

"So you don't have feelings for him anymore?" Max asks.

Right to the point. I don't want to lie, but I don't want to ruin things with him either.

"We're never going to be together. Jake doesn't want anything serious. At least not with me anyway. So I'm moving on."

"Fair enough."

When Max grabs my hand I can feel my stomach clench, and not in a good way. It feels wrong having someone other than Jake touch me.

But I don't want to ruin the only date I've had since high school so I don't say anything.

It doesn't take long to get to the Old Town Theater. It's on the opposite end of town from Haymakers, but still less than ten minutes from my house.

"It's not too crowded," Max comments when we pull into the parking lot.

"They only show one movie and it's not even a new one. Most people have probably already gone into the city to see it when it first came out. The theater stays open because some of the older folks in town don't like to drive into the city, so they see the movies here, and the high school kids come here on Friday and Saturday nights to make out."

He raises an eyebrow. "Is that a proposition?"

"But it's not Friday or Saturday night," I tease.

Max purchases the tickets and then offers to get me any snacks my heart desires.

"I've always loved the chocolate covered raisins," I admit.

He touches his chest. "A woman after my own heart. I love them too."

He buys two large boxes of the chocolate raisins, enough candy to feed a small army, and two large sodas, also enough for an army.

"I guess I didn't realize large would be quite so big." He laughs.

"It's an Old Town thing. They like to give people their money's worth. Everything here that's large is very large."

"Good to know. I'll store that away for future reference."

I'm always working so I don't get to the theater very often. It's not like I have anyone to go with anyway. I have to laugh when I see that the movie stars Katie Lawrence.

"I don't think this is supposed to be a comedy," Max whispers.

"I know Katie Lawrence," I whisper back.

He gives me a narrow-eyed glance like he doesn't believe me. I probably wouldn't believe me either.

"She's dating Jake's brother," I elaborate.

"Seriously?"

"Seriously."

When the only other person in the theater, Old Man Russell, who is like 100-years-old, turns around and gives us the stink-eye, Max and I both look at each other like little kids who have just been scolded by the teacher. Then we laugh and settle into our seats.

I don't pay much attention to the movie. I'm too busy thinking about what's going to happen after the movie when I have a feeling Max is going to try to kiss me. No one but Jake has kissed me since I graduated high school.

Max already has my hand in his. He's been playing with my fingers and lightly massaging my hand with his fingertips. Not that it doesn't feel good, maybe a little too good, but that's also the problem. I'm not sure I want it to feel good.

Once the lights come on Old Man Russell makes a point of glaring at us before he waddles out of the theater.

"So what did you think?" Max asks as he grabs my hand and laces our fingers together.

"Of the movie or the company?" I tease.

"Both."

"The movie was a little too dramatic for my taste. I prefer action or comedy. I liked the company much better."

"Good to know," he replies.

"And what did you think?" I throw the question back at him.

"I liked the movie. But I have a thing for drama. One of my majors in college was literature. And the movie was actually based on a short story by W.W. Jacobs."

"Interesting. And what about the company?"

He gives me a big grin. "I liked that even better."

As we step outside the night couldn't be more perfect. The sky is a blanket of sparkling stars and the moon is radiant and full.

"Is there someplace we could get coffee?" Max asks as he glances down the small main street where everything has been closed for hours.

"Not in Old Town."

I can see the disappointment cross his face.

"I'd invite you back to my place for a drink, if I actually had a place, but I'm still crashing with my sister for the moment. She's a very light sleeper."

"I don't think my parents would appreciate you coming over this late either."

"I had a really great time." When Max looks into my eyes I can feel it coming. The kiss. The air between us has a little bit of extra electricity as he leans over and touches his lips to mine.

Just as he's about to deepen the kiss a car horn blast fills the air. We both jump back as the horn continues to blare.

"What's going on?" Max looks around confused.

I'm not as confused. I immediately spot Jake's truck parked across the street. He's obviously been watching us since we got out of the movie theater and he laid on his horn as soon as Max tried to kiss me.

"I can't believe this," I practically yell as I stomp across the street to Jake's pickup.

I pound on the driver's side window until he opens in for me.

"What do you think you're doing?" I scream.

"I'm watching you," he yells back.

"You have no right to do that!"

"Last time I checked this was a free country." He glares at me. "And you don't own Main Street."

"You can't just follow me on my date." I'm so angry I'm practically spitting. "It's an invasion of privacy."

I can feel Max come up behind me and place his hand on the small of my back. "Is everything okay?" He asks the question loud enough for Jake to hear it.

"I just want to make sure you're okay," Jake makes a point of looking at Max. "You don't really know this guy."

"Harley's dad didn't have an issue with me taking his daughter on a date," Max says.

Jake's eyes narrow to angry slits. "He met your dad?"

I nod. "And my dad likes him. Which is more than I can say for you."

"Her mom made me cookies," Max rubs it in.

I bite back a grin. I know if I laugh it will really piss Jake off.

"How do you know he's not some psycho-killer? Everyone loved Ted Bundy too before he killed them."

"Do I look like a psycho-killer?" Max actually sounds a little hurt by the accusation.

"You're being completely ridiculous, Jake. He's not a psycho-killer. You have nothing to worry about. His sister works at Tawnee Mountain. His uncle owns the resort."

Jake stammers, "He what?" at the exact same moment Max says, "How did you know?"

I give Max a quick smile then turn my attention back to Jake. "You need to go back to Haymakers. It's not even close to closing time. How could you leave Tucker and Gracie alone?"

Jake frowns. "It's a slow night."

"I don't care if it's slow. Gracie is pregnant, remember?"

"I had to make sure you were okay." Jake looks crestfallen. Like a puppy that's just been beaten by its owner.

"I'm fine. Now leave."

He points a finger in Max's direction. "If I find out you've done anything to hurt her I'll beat that big smile right off your face."

"I'm not smiling," Max says.

"When you do smile it's really big," Jake clarifies.

"I'm not sure if that's an insult or a compliment," Max says.

Jake shakes his head. "Just don't hurt her."

"I would never do anything to hurt anyone and I certainly would never hurt Harley."

Jake starts his engine and pulls away without another word. But he does take one quick look back at me before he disappears into the night.

The drive to my house it unbearably quiet. I'm completely mortified and not sure what to say. Maybe Max doesn't know what to say either. He's probably never been stalked by his date's ex before.

Not that Jake is even my ex. Don't you have to be someone's boyfriend before you can be her ex?

Max parks in my parent's driveway and turns off his engine. I take that as a good sign. If he left the engine running that would mean he probably didn't want to see me again.

When he turns to face me he isn't smiling. I take that as a not-so-good sign. But then he takes my hand in his and I feel a little hopeful again.

"So how did you know about my uncle?"

I laugh. "This is Old Town. Everyone knows everything about everybody. If you're going to live here you'd better get used to it. Why didn't you tell me?"

He shrugs. "I don't want everyone to know I'm a trust fund baby. I don't actually have access to my family's vast fortune now anyway. My mom and my uncle want me and my sister to work for a living and not have everything handed to us on a silver platter."

"Stuff like that doesn't matter to me anyway," I tell him.

"Why'd you agree to go out with me?" he asks.

"Because you asked," I admit.

"That's all it takes? Here I thought it was my good looks and charm."

"Those certainly help." I heave a sigh. "Most guys in town don't want to mess with the Wilde brothers. For obvious reasons. And they know Jake and I were together for a while."

He raises an eyebrow, "A while?"

"A long while."

"And you're sure you're not still together."

"I'm sure."

"Is Jake sure?"

I shake my head. "I'm not so sure."

"I'd really like to see you again," Max says.

"But?"

He laughs. "You're perceptive."

"One of my many talents. Would you like to see me juggle?"

"I think I already saw that at Haymakers when you carried over my meal, several condiments and my beer all at the same time."

"It's a feat I perform every night."

"I really think you need to get things sorted out with Jake first. The guy seems to be going a little nuts."

"After everything he's put me through he deserves it."

Max's expression turns serious again. "Are you sure you're over Jake?"

I nod even though I'm not sure at all.

But I want to be over him. I need to be over him. I need to get on with my life. So I lean over to kiss Max.

I'm surprised when he doesn't hesitate to kiss me back. I want the kiss to be magical and fireworks-inducing, but the only thing that I see is the look on Jake's face as he drove away tonight.

Like someone had just stolen his best friend.

***

It's almost impossible for me to get to sleep. I toss and turn, but I can't get the image of Jake out of my mind. I'm still angry, but I'm also hurt. And I also feel bad that Jake seems to be hurting too.

What are we doing to each other?

For the first time ever I actually dread going into work tomorrow. Ever since I started working at Haymakers I couldn't wait to get into work. I normally can't wait to see Jake and the rest of the Wilde boys and their girls.

Now it's making my stomach knot thinking about seeing him. Maybe my parents are right. Maybe it's best if they sell their house and I leave Old Town for good.

But I never imagined myself anywhere but in Old Town. And I never imagined myself with anyone but Jake Wilde.

Truth be told, even with everything that's happened, I still can't imagine myself ever being with anyone else.

Does that make me pathetic, or a real fool for love? Probably both.

I get out of bed and make my way over to my large bedroom window. It faces the Wilde's house and I can see Jake's bedroom window from mine. For years I used to stare out my window and watch Jake's bedroom. It's too far away to make out any details, but I could see whether his bedroom light was off or on. I'd always try to imagine what he was doing. I used to imagine him lying in his bed thinking about me. I know now that was probably wishful thinking. Even when he was with other girls I hoped he was still thinking about me.

Like I said, pathetic.

I notice his bedroom light is on. For the first time ever I don't have that sinking feeling in the pit of my stomach that he has another girl with him. I know he's alone.

I just wonder what it means…

Ten

Jake

I know I look like shit, but Tucker will kill me if I call in sick to work again. I didn't get more than a few minutes sleep the entire night. I kept seeing that beach boy with his hand on Harley's sexy back. Him kissing her luscious pink lips. Him holding her delicate hand in his. It's like an endless loop that just keeps playing over and over in my mind.

I never thought it would feel like this. I feel like I've been completely gutted and there's nothing left but a hallow shell of a man.

The image staring back at me in the mirror scares the shit out of me. He looks more like one of those movie zombies than an actual human being. The only thing that's missing is some foaming of the mouth, but I'm sure I'll have that covered before the dinner shift.

I take one more look out my bedroom window. I'm not sure what I'm hoping to see. I can just about see Harley's bedroom from mine. I never told her that I used to always watch out the window to make sure she got home okay. Even nights when I had another girl over I'd find some kind of excuse to look out the window when I knew she was on her way back. Maybe I should have told her.

Maybe I should have done a lot of things. Like take her out on a real date. She looked so happy with that beach boy. She was smiling and laughing. Taking her to a movie would have been such a simple thing to do, but I never bothered.

Maybe because I didn't want things between us to be real. If we went on a date I would have had to admit that we had a relationship. I would have had to admit that I love her. That I've always loved her and always will love her.

I wanted to let her go. I wanted her to have someone better than me. I wanted her to have a better life than I could ever give her.

But I can't seem to live without her. It's literally killing me.

The problem is that I did too good a job of pushing her away and I'm afraid now that I'll never be able to get her back.

When I enter the kitchen both Gracie and Tucker look up from their breakfast plates and stare at me. Gracie looks worried and Tucker looks pissed.

Maybe it will be a typical day after all.

I pour a cup of black coffee and sit at the table.

"You look like shit," Tucker greets me.

"Do you want something to eat?" Gracie asks.

"Thanks." I glare at Tucker. "I'm not hungry," I reply to Gracie.

"You should try to eat something." Gracie's voice is so soft it's hard to hear her sometimes.

"I can't eat." My stomach is one gigantic knot just thinking about what Harley is going to say when she sees me. In my worst nightmares she tells me that she's quitting Haymakers, leaving Old Town and never coming back.

Of course that's what I always thought I wanted to happen. I didn't realize it would destroy me when it did.

"Is Harley working tonight?" Tucker asks.

I shrug. "I hope so."

His eyes narrow. "What do you mean you hope so? You're her boss, remember. You need to know whether she's working or not."

"I did something really stupid last night."

"Shocking," Tucker retorts.

"I followed her on her date."

"You did what?" His voice seems to have raised an octave. I just hope he doesn't hit me. I'm not sure I could even fight back in my current state.

"I followed her. I had to make sure she was okay. She doesn't really know that guy. I thought he might be some psycho."

Tucker rises from the chair and crosses his thick arms over his massive chest. "Seriously, Dude. You need help. And that says a lot coming from me."

Gracie hurries to grab their plates from the table. "He's not a psycho. His uncle owns the Tawnee Mountain Resort."

I shake my head. "How is it possible that everyone knows that but me?"

Tucker points a finger at me. "Gracie and I are having a baby. Don't do anything to screw up Haymakers, got it? We need that income."

I nod. "I got it."

"Good. Now pull yourself together and get to work."

***

As usual Harley is waiting for me outside Haymakers. She looks as beautiful as ever. I just wish I could make her smile the way I used to. I wish I could make her eyes light up again when she sees me, but they don't.

"I'm sorry," I mumble, and I'm actually surprised by the words that have come out of my mouth.

"What?" She seems just as surprised as I am.

"I'm sorry I followed you. But I did want to make sure you were okay."

She nods, but doesn't say anything else. I unlock the front door and we both head inside.

Haymakers is eerily quiet as we both ready the place for the first customers, our lunch regulars.

Tucker and Gracie make their way inside a few minutes after we do, but neither of them are in a talkative mood either.

There's a tremendous amount of tension in the air between all of us. Luckily the regulars don't seem to notice as they stream in for their lunches.

I watch as Harley waits on her tables, and jokes around with the patrons who have been coming in for years. She looks happy. I guess I never realized how much she seems to enjoy her job. And she's a natural at it. I always assumed she'd want more, and that she deserved a lot more, instead of thinking about how much she already has right in front of her. I never really listened when she told me that working at Haymakers and being with me were the two things that made her happiest.

It takes every ounce of restraint I have not to grab her by the hand and pull her into the back room with me. I want her more than I've ever wanted her in my life. I have an overwhelming desire to be with her, to be inside her, and to make her mine again.

Mine.

I guess it's true that you never really appreciate what you have until it's gone.

I want her back more than I want to breathe. I think I might have a shot until I see the beach boy waltz in and take a seat at one of Harley's tables.

My heart sinks when I see her face light up when she spots him. When she practically runs over to greet him I feel like I've been punched in the gut. I've never wanted to hurt anyone as much as I want to hurt Max Elliot. I'm sure he's a great guy, even if he sticks out like a sore thumb in Old Town. But I hate the way Harley looks at him, and I hate the way she smiles at him and I hate the way she's touching his arm as they talk.

"Is everything okay?" Tucker asks.

I turn to my brother and frown. "Why would you ask that?"

"Gee, I don't know. You seem awfully interested in watching Harley and the beach boy."

"I don't like him."

"You don't like him or you don't like the fact that Harley likes him?"

"Both."

"What are you going to do about it?"

"You mean besides killing him?" I say it as a joke, but Tucker isn't laughing. He doesn't even crack a smile.

Then to my complete and utter surprise my brother Cooper hurries into Haymakers. Unless there's some kind of emergency he only hangs out at Haymakers on the weekends because he lives in Manhattan and works on Wall Street.

114

He's obviously not working today because he's dressed in casual clothing and he's at the bar in the middle of the day.

"Is there something wrong?" I ask as Cooper heads over to the bar. He's not someone who smiles very much anyway, but today he's looking particularly grim.

"Why don't you tell me?" he fires back. He's obviously not in a very good mood.

When Cooper and Tucker exchange glances it occurs to me that perhaps Tucker's responsible for Cooper's little surprise visit to Old Town. Tucker probably phoned him to tell him he was worried about me.

"What did Tucker say?" I stare at Cooper.

"He told me he was worried about you. You look like shit, by the way. He wasn't exaggerating at all."

"Thanks a lot," I glare at Tucker.

"We're all in this together," Tucker shoots back.

He's right. Even though I'm the one who managers Haymakers each of the Wilde brothers is a co-owner of the bar.

"It's obvious things have gone too far," Cooper says. "So one of two things is going to happen. You're either going to tell Harley you love her, make some kind of commitment to the girl and finally stop the parade of women through the back room for good, or you're going to fire her and tell her never to come back to Haymakers."

I wipe the sweat that is beginning to trickle down my temples. "I'll take care of it."

Cooper narrows his gaze at me. "When?"

"Tonight. I promise."

"What are you planning on doing?" Cooper looks unconvinced at the veracity of my promise.

"I really messed things up," I admit. "I'm going to have to make a grand gesture. Something I know will win her back."

He holds up an index finger. "You've got one night. If things aren't worked out Tucker is going to fire her and forbid her from ever stepping foot in Haymakers again. Got it?"

I swallow. I can tell by the stern looks on both my brothers' faces that they're both dead serious.

"I got it."

"Good." Cooper takes a seat at the bar. "Now get me a beer. That was a really shitty bumper-to-bumper ride through the tunnel."

The rest of the afternoon goes by in kind of a blur. When we get slammed with a busload of retirees doing some kind of antique tour through rural New Jersey Cooper rolls up his sleeves and gives us a hand serving.

"Are you planning on hiring anyone else?" he asks as he pours several beers.

"Eventually," I reply.

He glances over at Gracie, who's taking a break with her feet up.

"She's getting awfully big. She may not be able to work too much longer."

I nod. "It's really hard to find good help."

"Maybe if you didn't screw everyone you hired," Tucker says. "We'd be able to keep some people."

"I'm done with that."

He purses his lips at me. "I'll believe it when I see it."

"Have you ever thought about hiring some guys?" Cooper suggests. "I can guarantee you won't be taking any of them into the back room."

"Do you have any suggestions where I might find some of these guys? They're not exactly beating down the door to work at Haymakers."

"You still talk to Coach Stanley? Maybe he knows some former football players who didn't end up going to college and are looking for work. They'd probably jump at the chance to work with Jake Wilde. You're still a legend at Old Town High."

I have to give Cooper credit. He does put every bit of his intelligence to good use.

"I'll give the Coach a call and see if he has some suggestions."

He gives me a nod then takes a tray of beers over to one of the tables.

It's well past the dinner rush when Cooper's better half finally arrives. He certainly hit the jackpot when he got Riley to accept his proposal. Not only is she a beauty, she's got the brains to match. The only woman I've ever met who's as gorgeous and brilliant as Riley is now standing next to me trying to get me to take a food order for her.

"Extra pickles. No ketchup. Got it?" Harley looks at me like I'm completely stupid.

"I've got it," I tell her.

"You don't look like you've got it."

"What makes you say that?"

"You haven't been yourself lately." She actually sounds concerned.

When our eyes meet there's a surge of energy between us and my heart swells. I wish she knew how much I miss her. She will very soon.

"You can count on me, Harley."

Her narrowed eyes are filled with uncertainty.

"Trust me," I tell her.

"I wish I could." She doesn't wait for me to respond. She just heads toward another table.

Riley looks surprised when I grab her arm. "I need your help."

"Okay." She sounds hesitant.

"I'm sure Coop mentioned that things with me and Harley are—um—strained."

She nods.

"I'm going to give her a song."

Her eyes widen. "You are?"

"Please make sure she sits down right next to the stage."

"Sure. Of course. But aren't you missing something? Like a band?"

"I'll be doing this alone. Just me and my guitar. Get Gracie to sit with her too."

Riley doesn't waste any time gathering up Harley and Gracie and the three of them move chairs next to the stage.

There are quite a few patrons in the place for a week night and they're all looking at the stage when they see the girls sit down on the chairs.

Tucker and Cooper both come up next to me. "Need a little back up?" Cooper offers.

"I've got it."

I normally don't play guitar when our band, Wilde Riders, gets together. I leave that up to Tucker and Cooper. But that doesn't mean I can't play. I know my way around a fretboard.

I hurry into my small office and grab my old Fender acoustic guitar. I leave it here for those rare occasions when I have a few spare minutes to play around with it.

I strum a few bars just to make sure it's still in tune.

"You can do this," I tell myself. I've been singing with Wilde Riders for nearly ten years. We've played in front of packed houses hundreds of times. But I've never felt so nervous. I actually feel like I'm going to puke.

I take in a deep breath to try and calm my nerves. "It's now or never."

With guitar in hand I head back out into the bar.

Harley is nervously looking around the bar, no doubt wondering what's up and where I disappeared. When her eyes catch mine her face turns from anxious to confused.

She whispers something to Riley but Riley just shakes her head in response.

When I glace over at my brothers who are now standing near the corner of the stage Cooper gives me a thumbs up sign.

The stage lights have already been turned on and I assume the microphone has been turned on as well. I hurry towards the stage before I change my mind or throw up.

As I look out at the small crowd that has now gathered near the stage my attention is drawn to Harley. She truly is the most amazing person in the world. And the fact that she once loved me seems like a miracle. One that I didn't appreciate enough.

If I can make her fall in love with me again it won't be something I take for granted, that's for damn sure.

"This Dan Fulton song is dedicated to Harley Davis. It's called Count On Me."

It'll be alright, I say
When you start to cry
But I know damn well that it's not true
Your fingers in my palm
I fight to keep you calm
But I know keeping calm's not what you do
And the words I choose are a useless few

You can count on me to let you down

'Cause I'm a cracking ledge
And I'm a broken bridge
I'm the tearing rope that you hang from
And you're a stranded soul
I leave beside the road
And throw a callous wave as I roll on
Or at the best I'll drive you half way home

You can count on me to let you down

You can count on me to let you down
I'll be the one to watch you slip and fall
I'll be the one to watch you hit the ground
I'll be the one who doesn't move at all
You can count on me to let you down

Once I finish singing the song the audience is eerily quiet. It's as if they're all wondering what just happened. Maybe Harley is too. She's staring at me with her mouth wide open.

Time feels like it's running at super-slow speed, like in action movies when they slow everything down enough for every movement to be seen.

I'm relieved when Cooper starts to applaud and the rest of the onlookers follow his lead.

I jump down from the stage and grab Harley's hand. I pull her into the back room with me and shut the door behind us.

She still looks dazed and confused. "You gave me a song." It's almost like she can't believe that I sang a song for her.

"I did."

"Why?"

It's not a question I was expecting. I'm not sure how to respond. "Because I want you, Harley. I want to be with you."

As I pull her close my heart is beating so fast I feel like it's going to beat right out of my chest. I gently stroke her cheek with my hand and it immediately calms my nerves.

Then I kiss her. Softly at first giving myself time to get reacquainted with her luscious lips. Then I deepen the kiss. I missed her taste, a hint of cherry like the lip gloss she always wears. I quickly lose myself in her presence. Just being near her again, smelling the scent of her shampoo and feeling her soft skin under my hand, it's my own personal Nirvana.

My dick has completely sprung to life, something I haven't felt in a while, not since I've been in my break-up funk. I want her to know how badly I want her. How much I've missed being with her. I grab her and push my throbbing erection against her.

"I want you," I whisper into her ear. "I need to be inside of you."

To my complete surprise she pushes me away. "No."

Now I'm the one who looks dazed and confused. "No?"

She shakes her head. "No. This isn't right."

Before I can say another word she opens the door and hurries out of my office.

I stand there for a few minutes in shock, trying to figure out what I did wrong.

Cooper and Tucker are standing at the bar waiting for me when I approach.

I do a quick scan of the place, but I don't see Harley anywhere. I don't see Riley or Gracie either. "Where'd the girls go?"

"Harley said she had to leave early," Cooper informs me. "And Riley and Gracie went with her."

"I need to find her." I know I sound a little frantic, but I can't help it. I feel completely out of control.

Tucker shakes his head and blocks my path. He knows there's no way I'll be able to get by him. "You're going to stay here and close the bar with us. All hands on deck with the girls gone."

"But…"

Both my brothers shake their heads.

"Now tell us what you said," Cooper demands.

I heave a sigh and try to remember exactly what I did say. I was so excited to have Harley in my arms again it's all kind of a blur.

"I told her I wanted her," I admit.

Cooper raises an eyebrow. "Anything else?"

I bite the inside of my cheek. I've never been able to break the nervous habit. "I think I said that I wanted to be inside of her."

Both of my brothers are now looking at me like I'm stupid.

"Please tell me you said more than that," Tucker urges.

I shrug. "She didn't give me a chance. She ran out of my office."

Cooper and Tucker both cross their arms over their chests at the same time and I get the sinking feeling they're going to start grilling me.

Tucker eyes me. "After your grand gesture of singing her a song that's the best you could do?"

"That's what I always say," I admit. "I guess it was just habit."

Now Cooper joins in. "You couldn't think of anything else to say? Something more appropriate for trying to win her back?"

I rub my temple. "I screwed up again, didn't I?"

"Majorly," Tucker says.

"You'll need to go all in," Cooper suggests.

"What do you mean?"

"I asked Riley to marry me. That's how I sealed the deal."

"I saved Gracie from her psycho ex-boyfriend and almost got killed in the process," Tucker adds. "But I wouldn't recommend that strategy."

"And considering I'm looking more and more like the psycho ex-boyfriend every day, it's probably best I pursue another tactic."

Cooper pats my back. "You'll have all night to think about it. The girls are staying with Harley tonight."

Great. Another sleepless night.

Eleven

Harley

"How is it possible that you've never had a sleepover party?" Riley asks as she pours the freshly popped popcorn into an extra-large bowl.

"Let's just say I was never very popular with the girls when I was in school. I was more of a tomboy and most of my friends were guys. Not very conducive to sleepovers."

"I think we now have everything we need." Riley inspects our comfort food. "Popcorn with extra butter; freshly baked chocolate chip cookies with extra chocolate chips and vanilla milkshakes with extra ice cream."

I take a sip of my milkshake. "This is really good. I think you missed your true calling, Riley. You should open an ice cream shop."

She laughs. "Maybe when Cooper and I get sick of life in Manhattan we'll retire to Old Town and open up a little shop in the town square."

"You need to make your first million first," I remind her.

She nods. "Do you want to grab the popcorn? I'll get the cookies and we can talk in the living room?"

"Sure." I grab the tub of popcorn and my milkshake and head into the living room.

Riley and I crash on the coach and Gracie takes the big chair my dad usually sits in when he watches football.

"Spill," Riley says between bites of popcorn.

"I'm not sure what to say."

"How about telling us what happened with Jake and why you ran out of Haymakers like the place was on fire."

"After he sang that song for you," Gracie adds.

I take in a deep breath and try my best not to cry. "I was over the moon when he sang that song for me. I thought it really meant something. But then when he took me into the back room, everything came crashing down around me. He treated me like I was a just another fifteen-minute fling. To say I was disappointed would be an understatement."

Riley pursues her lips like she's giving it some thought. "I'm not trying to defend Jake. I know he can be a womanizing asshole. But I really do think he loves you. Maybe he just doesn't know how to say it. I get the feeling he doesn't have much experience in that department."

I blink back tears. "Do you really think he loves me?"

She nods. "Obviously I haven't known him as long as you have, but something has changed. And I've never seen him look so—I don't know—defeated. Even when he was in danger of losing the bar, he didn't look like he looks now."

"He looks like a little boy who lost his one and only friend," Gracie interjects.

That strikes me right in the gut. It's the same thought I had the night Jake saw me on my date with Max.

"My parents want to sell the house," I admit. "I have to make a decision whether I want to stay here and buy it from them, or leave Old Town and do something else with my life."

"You can't leave." Gracie looks panic-stricken.

126

I never even considered how leaving would impact the rest of Jake's family, particularly Gracie and Riley, who have become the closest thing to sisters I've ever had.

Gracie and I have talked about me being there with her and Tucker when the baby is born since she doesn't have a mom to support her. Not that Tucker won't spoil her rotten, but it's not quite the same thing as having another female in your corner.

"I don't want to leave," I admit. "The only thing I've ever wanted was to be married to Jake and help him run Haymakers. It's been my dream since I was a teenager. It's the only thing I could ever see doing with my life. It's the only thing that makes me truly happy. I'm just not sure that I'm what makes Jake happy."

"Well he's sure unhappy when he doesn't have you," Gracie says. "I'm actually worried about him."

"So are Cooper and I," Riley adds. "I know you didn't actually ask for my advice, but can I give it to you?"

I smile. "The two of you are probably the only people on the planet whose advice I would take."

"Good. I think you should give Jake another chance to get things right."

I take in a deep breath and slowly exhale. "One more chance. But he better not screw things up this time."

Riley laughs. "I think Cooper and Tucker would kill him if he did."

"Enough of the girl talk," I say. "We need to raise the level of testosterone in this room before I start to get sick. How about a Jason Statham movie night? I've got all of the Transporter movies on my iCloud."

***

I know I need to have a conversation with Max. It's not fair to leave him waiting and wondering if anything is going to happen between us. I'm glad I had the chance to go out with him. I got the chance to see what it would be like to be with someone other than Jake Wilde.

Too bad Max pales in comparison.

Don't get me wrong, he's a great guy. He's just not Jake.

"Max," I say when he answers his cell phone.

"Harley Davis." He sounds surprised to hear from me. "How are you doing?"

"I'm okay…"

"That doesn't sound very convincing."

I take in deep breath. "I wanted to phone before you heard any rumors. Old Town is like a gossip mill."

"Let me guess. You're getting back together with your boy-friend."

"You are smart, but he was never really my boyfriend."

"But you want him to be, don't you?"

"Yes," I admit.

"And I get the feeling he wants you."

I laugh. "What makes you say that?"

"My first clue was when he followed us on our date. He was very possessive. I got the feeling that he already thought you were his."

"He's got some work to do," I admit. "But I think his heart is in the right place."

"Does he make you happy?" Max asks.

I think about it for a few seconds. "For the most part."

"Just make sure he treats you right. Make sure he treats you like you deserve to be treated."

"And how's that?"

"You're special, Harley. You've got a smile that lights up the room. Just make sure he appreciates what he's got if you decide to let him have you."

"I will," I promise.

"And if you ever want to participate in a ghost tour, just let me know. It's on the house."

I laugh. "I may take you up on that someday."

Twelve

Jake

"Don't mess things up again," Cooper says as he throws some banana slices in the blender for his morning smoothie.

"Or we'll have to kill you," Tucker adds as he pours himself a cup of coffee. "And I'm not kidding."

"I know. I won't."

I got zero sleep because I've been rehearsing what I want to say all night. I know this is my last shot to salvage things with Harley. If I mess this up I'll lose her forever.

And I can't imagine living a life without Harley in it.

I sit down at the small kitchen table. Tucker takes a seat next to me and Cooper sits down across from us.

"Tucker and I were talking..." Cooper says.

"Should I be nervous?" I ask.

They eye each other than Cooper continues, "We always said that the Wilde brother who started a family first would take the house."

I look back and forth between my brothers. "You're getting married, Coop. And you're having a baby, Tuck. So which one of you is going to call dibs on the house?"

Tucker clears his throat. "It looks like Gracie and I will be getting married with Cooper and Riley."

I furrow my brow. "Since when?"

"Since the girls decided they wanted a double wedding," Cooper replies. "And you know what Riley and Gracie want, Riley and Gracie get."

"Thanks for keeping me in the loop," I say sarcastically.

"You haven't exactly been firing on all cylinders lately," Tucker reminds me.

"Riley and I are going to be in New York for a while. We don't know what's going to happen with you and Harley…"

"I'm going to get her back," I assure them.

"I hope so," Cooper says. "But we know Tucker and Gracie are going to have a baby. So I think we should consider giving them the house."

"I don't want to admit that I'm a tad bit jealous. I'm the oldest. I always imagined I'd be the one to get the house. The one raising his family in the same place in which I grew up."

"It's not like you all won't be here all the time anyway," Tucker says. "Gracie and I will just be the ones living here on a daily basis."

I take in a deep breath then exhale. "Fine. Take the house."

Tucker pats my shoulder. "This means a lot to me, Big Bro. And it means a lot to Gracie."

"I expect to play Uncle Jake on a regular basis."

Tucker nods. "We probably need to start thinking about getting a nursery ready. I have no idea what any of that shit entails."

"I'm sure you'll find out very quickly," Cooper jokes.

"When do you want me out?" I ask.

Tucker frowns. "It's not like that. The baby isn't due until the holidays."

I nod. "I guess I'll start looking for an apartment or something. Maybe one of those places over on Third Street." There are several small apartment buildings a few blocks from Haymakers. I could easily walk to work from there.

Thirteen

Harley

It takes me a moment to realize there's someone standing over me. I wipe my eyes and look up at Jake. "What are you doing here?"

"Can we talk?"

"I think I've said all there is to say."

"Please."

That's a word that doesn't come out of Jake's mouth very often.

"Is there room on that tree for me?" He sounds desperate.

I move over just enough for him to sit on the tree next to me.

"I can't believe you're crying," he comments.

"I can't believe you're sitting here next to me so I guess that makes us even."

Jake lets out a single laugh. "We'll never be even. But you already know that."

I glance over at him. I've never seen him so solemn in my life. Jake's Mr. Charisma. The guy who lights up a room with his smile. Now he looks like a little kid who's dog died. "What are you doing here, Jake?"

He swallows. Jake Wilde is rarely at a loss for words. Then he bites the side of his cheek for a few moments before he takes in a deep breath. "Why haven't you left Old Town?"

I frown. "Because I've got a job at Haymakers."

He shakes his head. "That's not what I mean. You were the smartest girl in your high school class. You were the Valedictorian."

I shake my head. "I was the Salutatorian. That's second best."

"You were still smart enough to give a speech at graduation. None of the Wilde boys ever did that. Not even Cooper. And he got a scholarship to Columbia."

"So? What's your point?" I don't like the direction this conversation is taking. I can feel my cheeks starting to burn and I'm sure they're getting red.

"You probably could have gotten a scholarship to any college in the country."

"I know," I admit. "Even though I insisted I wasn't going to college, my guidance counselor, Mr. Little made me apply anyway. I got accepted everywhere I applied and got a number of scholarships."

"Why didn't you go?"

"You know why, Jake."

I look into his eyes. When I see how much pain he's in it tugs on my heartstrings.

I can see him start to blink back tears. I've seen Jake cry twice. First at his mom's funeral and then at his dad's. "I just wanted you to go. You deserve so much more than me, Harley. You know I'm never going to be anything but the manager of Haymakers. It's in my blood. As my dad always told me, it's what I was born to do. But it's not what I want for you. You're brilliant and so beautiful it hurts to even look at you. Why would you want to spend your life with someone like me? You could have so much more. You could go anywhere in the world. You could be anything. Why would you want to waste your life with someone like me?"

"Jake, why don't you let me decide what I want to do with my life?"

"Don't you want to go to law school? Or medical school? Don't you want to go to New York like Riley and Cooper? Or to LA like Hunter?"

I shake my head.

"But why?"

"You know why."

He bites his cheek again.

"One of these days you're going to bite your way through your cheek to the other side. Then what's going to happen? You'll have a hole in your face. That's what."

That breaks the tension in the air just a bit and we both laugh.

When he looks at me again, his expression is serious. "I don't deserve you."

"You're right. But I still love you."

"You told me you hated me."

"Is that why you decided to follow me on my date with Max? Because Jake Wilde can't stand the thought of anyone not adoring him."

He shakes his head. "I realized I can't stand the thought of you not loving me. Just you, Harley"

"I've always loved you, Jake. And I hope you realize I always will. That's why I couldn't leave and that's why I'll never leave. Because you're here."

"I don't want you to stay in Old Town just because of me."

"I'm not. I'm staying because I want to. It's my life. And it's my choice. I love working at Haymakers and I'm really good at it. Maybe it was what I was born to do too. Did you ever think of that?"

"I just don't want you to ever regret it."

"It may be a little too late for that."

"I know. I'm sorry. You were right. I knew that being with Regina would piss you off. I thought it would be the thing that would finally get you to leave. So you could have a real life."

"Being here in Old Town. Being with you. It is a real life."

"Obviously not much of one."

"Well maybe if you'd quite being such a prick."

When he doesn't reply I think maybe my big mouth might have pushed the wrong button. He stands and then extends his hand to me. "Would you hold this for me while I take a walk?"

I smile and grab his hand. Even in the most difficult of situations he has no trouble pulling out a pick up line.

I think he might take me to his house, but instead we head toward mine. "Are your parents still at the Bike Rally?"

I nod. "For a few days."

"Good."

"Why?"

"Because I want to see your bedroom."

Of course, Jake and all of the Wilde boys have been inside my house many times, but Jake has never been inside my bedroom. No guy except my dad has ever set foot inside there. My dad made sure of that.

"I don't want us inside my bedroom anymore," he adds after another round of cheek chewing.

That's about the weirdest thing I've ever heard. I've been inside Jake's bedroom a lot. As have most of the females in Old Town.

"I want a fresh start. One that doesn't include my bedroom."

I narrow my gaze. "What does that mean?"

"It means I'm finally going to try to be the man you deserve."

"Would you be a little more specific?" I don't want to jump to any conclusions. I also want him to say out loud what I think he's trying to say.

He stops and grabs my other hand so he's holding both of them. "If you're really not going to leave despite all of my best efforts to run you out of town. If you insist on sticking with me despite my many flaws. If this is the life you really want. Me and Haymakers. Then you deserve to have all of me."

I can feel tears start to run down my cheeks again as Jake places a soft kiss on each one of my knuckles.

"For being such a tough chick, you're sure doing a lot of crying," he teases.

I move to wipe the tears from my cheeks, but Jake beats me to it. He carefully wipes them away with his thumb. I've seen Tucker wipe the tears from Gracie's face and I've seen Cooper wipe tears from Riley's cheeks, but I never considered Jake to be the kind of sensitive and caring guy who would do something like that.

And now he's doing it for me.

Is it possible that he really does care about me after all?

"Come on," he says as he pulls me toward my house.

My bedroom is messier than I'd like. But when I left this morning, I never in a million years thought I'd have anyone in here. Especially not Jake Wilde.

The room is a strange mashup of teenage girl fantasy stuff left over from my high school days and more serious decorations that reflect my foray into womanhood. My parents always allowed me to decorate my own room and the eclectic mixture of colors and styles reflects the various stages of my coming-of-age.

"It's exactly how I imagined it," Jake says as he glances around.

"You imagined what my bedroom looked like?" I laugh. "I find that hard to believe."

"Why?" He's actually serious.

I roll my eyes. "Like you care about my bedroom."

He grabs my elbow and pulls me close. "I think about everything to do with you, Harley Davis. I think about your bedroom. I think about what you're doing at night when you're not with me. I think about what you eat in the mornings. Every day I wonder what you'll be wearing when you walk into Haymakers. I think about you all the time."

I gulp. It never occurred to me that Jake thought about me at all except when he was horny. "But why? Why would you think about what I was eating for breakfast? Or what I was going to wear every day?"

When our eyes meet, Jake's gaze is so intense, it nearly sucks all the breath right out of my lungs. "You know why, Harley."

I shake my head. "I don't."

He pulls me so close that I can feel his breath on me. "You have no idea?"

"None."

"Because I love you. I've always loved you. I just wanted you to have more. I wanted you to have everything you deserve. And I knew that was way more than I could ever offer."

"I only want you, Jake. That's all I ever wanted."

"I just hope it's not too late. For me to give you everything you want."

"I just want you."

"Are you sure I'm enough? That Haymakers is enough?"

I nod. "I'm sure."

When Jake kisses me, it's almost like a first kiss. It's tentative and tender. He's never kissed me that way before.

"I want things to be different," he says as he strokes my cheek.

They already are. A lot different. "How?"

"Just you and me. From now on."

"Just to be clear. You're talking about sex."

He laughs. "I don't want to be with anyone but you. And yes, I am talking about sex."

"Are you sure?"

"What do I need to do? Give you a ring to prove it?"

That stops me cold. Surely, he's kidding. "No."

He looks confused. "No?"

I shake my head. "I don't need a ring to prove anything. I know things will be different."

"But are you saying you wouldn't take my ring. I mean, if I ever asked?"

"I'm not saying that. But you didn't ask and you don't have a ring so it's kind of a moot point."

He's giving me a weird look. Like I've given him some kind of challenge. "You know we've got not one but two Wilde weddings in just a few weeks."

"I'm well aware of that. I'm a bridesmaid in the first wedding and the maid of honor in the second. I've been doing a lot of dress shopping."

He nods. But I can tell by the expression on his face the conversation may be over for now, but it's far from completely over.

When he removes my bracelet from his pocket I cringe. I'm a little embarrassed that I threw it in his face. It was my most prized possession. I know it's not even worth that much monetarily, but it meant everything because it was from Jake.

Without saying anything he takes my left arm and hooks the bracelet back in place. "Don't take it off again."

I swallow. I've never seen him so serious in my life.

He holds up his arm and I see he's wearing the bracelet I bought him for Christmas. "I've never taken mine off, Harley."

I'm not sure what to say. It's a lot to process. All this time Jake was trying to push me away. To get to me leave Old Town because he thought I deserved more. All this time I questioned whether he cared about me at all and he actually loved me.

"We probably need to get ready for work," he suggests, and it urges me out of my thoughts.

"Yeah," I agree, but I know I sound surprised. I guess I expected Jake to go for a quickie like he always does.

He leans down and gives me another kiss. This one is a bit more passionate and charged. I can feel the heat shoot right down to my toes.

"Do you want to ride with me to Haymakers?"

140

Jake has never given me a ride to Haymakers. He always takes his own car in case he wants to pick someone else up. It takes me a few seconds to remember that he's not going to be picking anyone up because we're together.

Like a real couple.

I'm still having trouble wrapping my head around it.

"Okay." I hear the word coming out of my mouth, but it feels like someone else is talking. I guess I'm still trying to come to terms with the idea of actually being together as a couple. It's something I've dreamed about since I was a teenager. Something I've longed for so long, I still can't believe it's real. I almost feel like I need to pinch myself.

"Is everything okay?" Jake asks. He looks concerned.

I nod. "I think it's just going to take a while for me to believe that we're together. Like dating. Or whatever. I don't even know what to call it."

He pulls me close and I can feel his erection pressing against me. "We're doing more than dating." His voice is hard and possessive. I've never heard that tone before. It both excites me and scares me a little.

He cups my face with his hands. "I'm yours, Harley. I hope you realize what that means. You have me. All of me. All yours. Now and always."

This time when he kisses me, the fire between us is so intense it's almost too much to bear. We're a mash of lips and teeth and tongues. It doesn't take long for our hands to join the party and we're all over each other.

141

Jake and I have been together more times than I can count, but this is so different in some many ways, it feels like a first time all over again.

"We're going to be late," I say breathlessly between kisses.

"Tucker and Gracie can handle it until we get there."

"Are you sure?" I can imagine the angry glare Tucker will give us if we show up late again.

"Very," he says as he begins to unbutton my blouse. "You need to be mine again. I want you to have me inside of you before we go to work. Every time you see me today I want you to think about us being together. And I want you to be yearning for tonight when we can be together again. I need to make sure I ruin you for every other man."

"Ruin away." I give him a sexy little grin.

"Do you have any idea what you do to me, Harley?" He continues to remove my blouse. "There's not a woman on the planet who is as beautiful and sexy as you are."

His kisses move from my mouth down my neck and then to my shoulder blades. "I want to kiss every inch of your body. I want to stake my claim on it."

And I let him do just that. After he carefully removes my bra he kisses around my breasts and then takes my nipple into his mouth and licks and sucks it until I feel it harden. My other nipple gets just as much attention and I let out a low moan in response.

"I'm just getting started," he whispers into my ear.

As he runs his finger along the line of my jeans then stops to play with my bellybutton he's rewarded with a shiver that runs down my body. He knows how sensitive my bellybutton is so he spends a few extra seconds there until I'm a quivering mess.

After he unbuttons my jeans he bends down to put kisses all over my belly. He pulls my jeans down just far enough that he can kiss each of my hips and makes a small pit stop to tickle my bellybutton with his tongue.

"Bed?" I suggest, almost breathlessly, because my knees have gone a little weak and I'm not sure how much longer I can stand up.

We both stare at my bed for a moment. No one but me has ever been in that bed. It seems like a great place for us to have our first time together as an actual couple.

When he looks into my eyes I feel like he's thinking the same thing. "You've still got your pants half on."

"And you've still got all of your clothes on."

"Let's remedy that situation."

He helps me out of my very tight jeans and then just looks at me for a few moments. Naked except for my thong.

"What?" I ask coyly.

He shakes his head. "I still can't believe you're mine. All mine."

"I've always been yours," I remind him.

He nods. "I was just too stupid to realize it."

I look him up and down. "You're still fully clothed."

"Not for long," he says as he unbuttons his shirt.

It only takes him a few seconds to get undressed and I'm rewarded with a hard-on that looks like it could cut glass.

"Wow." I can't seem to keep my eyes off his erection. I can feel myself growing wet with anticipation. It's been over a week since we were together and for us that's a really long time.

Besides this feels completely different. I'm actually a little nervous. Butterflies have taken over my stomach.

He closes the small distance between us and pushes my thong down so he can have full access to the rest of my body.

As he kisses me he moves his fingers inside of me. "You're already so wet," he whispers.

"And you're already so hard," I tease.

"I'm glad you can see how badly I want you. How much I need to be inside of you right now."

I gasp when he lifts me into his arms and places me on the bed. He looks at me again for a long moment before he gets into bed with me.

I'm a little surprised that he hasn't reached for a condom. It's usually like a reflex for him. He always grabs one out of his pocket before his jeans come down.

"Are you forgetting something?" I hint.

When he shakes his head I swallow...hard. Then I wonder if he's thinking the same thing I'm thinking. "I'm not on the pill."

"It's okay," he whispers into my ear. "I want us to be together without any barrier between us. I want to feel you. I want you to feel me." Then with a seductive grin he adds, "And I want you to carry a part of me with you all day."

"But I'm not on birth control," I say again just to be sure he completely understands what I'm saying.

He narrows his eyes at me. "I heard you the first time you said it."

"What if I get pregnant?" I know it's kind of a mood breaker, but the question is important.

"Is it wrong of me to hope you do? That we can make a baby together."

I look into his eyes just to make sure he's serious. "Kind of. This is all happening so fast."

"In some ways it feels like it hasn't happened fast enough."

He has a point. We've known each other our whole lives and we've been sleeping together for well over a year.

He places his hand on my cheek. "I'll get a condom right now if you want me to. Just say the word. I'll do whatever you want me to do. I just want you to know I'm in this for the long haul. I hope you realize what that means. You're stuck with me for good."

I nod. "Okay."

He raises an eyebrow. "Okay?"

I take in a deep breath. "You don't have to use a condom."

He smiles. I don't ever think I've seen him look happier. "I want you to know that I've never been with anyone else without a condom. You're my one and only."

"Let's keep it that way," I tease.

"You have me, Harley. All of me. Now and always."

I look deep into his beautiful eyes and I know he's telling the truth. "I need you, Jake."

I don't have to say the words twice. He pulls me close and kisses me, a needy and voracious kiss. Soon our hands are all over each other's bodies again and we quickly become a tangle of heated body parts.

"I need to be inside of you," Jake practically growls.

"Yes, please," I reply just as hungrily.

I take in a sharp breath as he pushes inside of me. I'm a little surprised by how different it feels, how good it feels, without a condom.

I assume Jake feels the same when he moans my name. Then he starts to push, harder and deeper, filling me with every inch of him.

I can't control my cries of pleasure and I realize I don't have to. We're not at his place with Wilde brothers in the next room. We're in my bedroom alone. My parents are gone for the weekend.

"Oh, God, Jake," I practically scream as he thrusts even harder and deeper than I ever imagined he could. It's like he's on a quest to completely and totally possess me.

Small beads of sweat drip down his face as he continues to pump with everything he has. I feel like I could scream, but no sound actually comes out of my throat. I'm too enraptured, too overwhelmed with the sensations, to even utter a word.

"Come with me, Harley," he commands.

I'm already gone as Jake gives one final hard thrust. I feel like I've burst into thousands of shooting stars, but he pulls me tight so I won't completely fall to pieces.

"I love you, Harley," he whispers in my ear.

"I love you too," I whisper back.

We both lie perfectly still for a few moments while we come back down to planet Earth.

Jake places a quick kiss on my nose. "I wish we could stay in bed together all day."

"Tucker would kill us both. And then still make our corpses work."

He runs his thumb down my cheek. He's got a bit of mischief in his eyes. Then he gives me a small smile. It's not one I've ever seen before. His smiles are always big and charismatic. This one isn't large, but it seems more genuine. "I want to take you on a real date. Dinner, a movie, maybe even making out in my truck."

"Why the sudden desire to go on a date? Not that I'm complaining. I'd love to go on an actual date with you."

"I saw how happy you looked when you were on a date with that beach boy."

I laugh. "Beach boy? Seriously? His name is Max."

He frowns. "I want you to look that happy but I want it to be with me."

I place my hand on his face. "You make me very happy, Jake. Just by telling me you want to be with me. Us being together. Actually dating. It's all I ever wanted."

When he swallows I can tell he wants to say more. I brace myself for what's about to come next. With Jake Wilde you never know…

"I want more."

I raise an eyebrow. "More?"

He nods. "We haven't worked out any of the details yet, but it looks like I'm going to be moving into an apartment. With Tucker and Gracie starting a family Cooper and I decided it was best for them to take the house. I want you to consider moving into the apartment with me."

When I shake my head he looks crestfallen. Like I just punched him. So I quickly add, "This is going to be my house. I'll be living here."

Now he looks confused. "What do you mean?"

"We haven't really had a chance to talk about it, but my parents sold the dealership. They're going to be traveling around Europe for a few years so they're giving me the house."

"Europe? Your parents don't even like to drive into New York City."

I shake my head. "I know. It's weird. It must be some kind of midlife crisis. I think when your mom and dad died they took it hard. My point is that this house is big enough for more than just me."

He gives me that small smile again. "Harley Davis, are you asking me to move in with you?"

I smile. "I guess maybe I am."

"Isn't that a little premature?" he teases. "We haven't even had our first date yet."

"Well we did just have sex before our first date too."

He laughs. It's good to see him laugh again. "We never did do anything the conventional way, did we?"

I shake my head. "Nothing about our relationship is conventional."

"I'm not sure I can be your boss anymore." He bites the side of his cheek nervously.

Now I'm nervous too. I never considered the idea of not working at Haymakers just because we're together. I love everything about my job.

"Maybe I should talk to my brothers about you being a co-manager with me. Maybe you could take over the books, everything on the computer. I never got the hang of all the accounting software Cooper installed. You were always good in math."

"I was good in every subject," I remind him. "And I have a feeling your brothers would love for me to take over the bookkeeping. Cooper would probably breathe a sigh of relief."

"Am I really that bad?"

We both laugh. Then he looks into my eyes. "I think we'll make a great team."

"I know we will," I assure him. Then I slap his naked butt. "Now get your ass into the shower and get dressed for work. If I'm now co-manager I'm not going to let you get away with any shenanigans, Mister."

He gives me a big grin as he gets out of the bed. "Give some people a little bit of power and it goes right to their heads."

"You know it," I fire back.

Fourteen

Jake

I take a swipe at the beads of sweat dripping down my forehead. I can't remember the last time I was so nervous. It's possible that I've *never* been this nervous. Not even when we were vying for the State Championship and the entire football team was counting on me to work my magic on the field.

I take one more look at myself in the foyer mirror. Without my old jeans and cowboy boots on I barely recognize myself. I'm wearing the only pair of khaki pants and dress shoes that I own. If my hair was curlier and darker I'd look more like Cooper than I do myself.

When I showed Riley, Cooper, Gracie and Tucker the engagement ring I bought for Harley they were more than happy to let us have the night off from work for our date.

"This is it," I say to myself in the mirror. My stomach knots when I think about the possibility of Harley not accepting my proposal. "There's only one solution to that problem. Don't give her the option to say no."

I take in a deep breath and head out the door.

"Jake Wilde," Harley's dad says when he opens the front door. He looks me up and down and then harrumphs before he lets me inside his house.

Harley's mom reacts to me a little more positively, but just a little. At least she has a fake smile plastered on her face. Harley's dad is just glaring at me.

I breath a small sigh of relief when Harley comes dashing down the stairs. She looks absolutely stunning in a beautiful flowered sundress and heels. The outfit makes her look like a classic beauty. It's such a departure from the normal sexy outfits she wears on a daily basis at the bar.

We both stare at each other for a long minute before she says, "You clean up nicely."

I smile. "So do you."

She grabs the hem of the dress and does a quick spin. "I wasn't sure about this outfit."

"You look absolutely amazing."

That brings a smile to her face. "Thanks."

Harley's dad clears his throat and it breaks the moment between me and the love of my life.

"Have her home before midnight," Mr. Davis says.

"Dad!" Harley protests. "You've known Jake since he was born."

"I know Jake alright. And that's exactly why I'm enforcing a curfew."

"It's not a problem," I say. "I'll have her home early."

Mr. Davis nods and I grab Harley's hand and pull her out the door with me.

I want our date to be perfect in every way. I don't want her ever to think about Max and that date they had again. When I open the passenger side of the truck she actually lets out a small gasp. I have a huge bouquet of sunflowers waiting for her in the passenger seat.

"Flowers? For me?"

"Of course."

She turns back and gives me a huge grin which completely undoes me. She actually looks happy again. Truly happy. And it's because of me.

I don't think either of us pays much attention to the movie. It's some kind of chick flick that neither of us has much interest in. We're both fans of action movies. Plus we're too busy holding hands and kissing.

For the first time it makes sense to me why people go to see movies on dates. A lot of foreplay can take place in a theater seat. Much more than you'd think.

As we walk out of the theater hand in hand Old Man Russell gives us a dirty look as he walks by.

"We weren't that loud, were we?" I whisper to Harley.

"He's just jealous," she whispers back and we both laugh.

We don't even bother to get back into my truck. The Thai restaurant is just a short walk away down Main Street.

I have to admit that the closer we get to the restaurant the more nervous I feel. My life is about to change forever.

I hope.

We just about make it inside before the place closes. They don't exactly post hours of operation on the front door. They usually just close whenever customers stop coming in.

I'm not a huge fan of Thai food, but it's the nicest restaurant in Old Town. Our other choices are a pizza place, a coffee and sandwich shop, or a diner.

Harley's says her favorite thing on the menu is Pad Thai so I order it for both of us. My stomach is so knotted I can hardly eat so I just play with the food on my plate and kind of pretend I'm eating it.

"Don't you like it?" she asks.

I take in a deep breath. "I'm not really that hungry."

She frowns.

"There's a reason," I add. I reach into the pocket of my pants and pull out a small velvet box.

Harley's eyes are as wide as saucers. "Oh, my God," she whispers.

I slide off of my chair and get down on one knee in front of her. Then I open the ring box.

She gasps when she sees the diamond.

"Marry me, Harley."

Tears are streaming down her face when I take the ring out of the box and place it on her ring finger.

"It's too much. That ring must have cost you a fortune."

I grin. "Those jewelry store commercials on television say you're supposed to spend three months' salary on an engagement ring."

"I think we may be paying you too much if you can afford a rock like this," she jokes.

"You're worth every penny."

Epilogue

Four Wilde Weddings

Harley

"Are you sure I look okay?" Gracie and I stare into the temporary full length mirror that I've set up in the back room just for the weekend. Most people have heard of the Hugh Grant romantic comedy *Four Weddings and a Funeral*. Well we've got Four Weddings and a Rural Bar to deal with.

"You look amazing," Gracie assures me.

She places one more tiny piece of baby's breath in my hair. I'm wearing an updo with accents of baby's breath. It's the perfect complement for the ivory embroidered dress I'm wearing. It's the same gown my mom wore for her wedding. She saved it for my big day.

It's Sunday night and we've closed Haymakers, except for the family and friends we've invited for our wedding. I have to thank them for their stamina. This is the fourth wedding most of them have attended in the past two days.

***

Yesterday Riley and Cooper got married in a beautiful ceremony at a local community church. They had the wedding Riley had always hoped for with the church service, the flowers, the attendants and the minister officiating. Cooper was over the moon when she walked down the aisle. Gracie was right about the dress she picked out. He was overwhelmed by the sight of her.

Then we got in our cars and hurried to the town square where Gracie and Tucker exchanged vows under a lovely gazebo at dusk. Tucker looked too happy to be scary. And Gracie's baby bump only made the ceremony more special.

We celebrated both of their weddings with a big reception at the Tawnee Mountain Resort compliments of Cooper and Riley's big Wall Street salaries. From the chocolate fountains to the fancy five course meal, they spared no expense for their big day.

This morning the Wilde brothers and their girls all snuck out to Buttermilk Falls with a non-denominational minister who specializes in outdoor weddings. We all successfully evaded the paparazzi for a super-secret wedding ceremony between Hunter and his movie star girlfriend, Katie Lawrence.

***

Now we're all gathered back at Haymakers for the final of the four Wilde weddings. If someone would have asked me even two months ago if I thought I'd be getting married to Jake Wilde I would have told them they were crazy.

But now it seems like the most obvious thing in the world.

It may seem a bit impulsive to propose to someone on a first date, but for Jake and I it felt like a long time coming when he finally popped the question. As I stared at the glimmering gemstone that he placed on my finger I wasn't sure that I could ever be any happier than I was at that moment.

But that moment is actually being topped by how I'm feeling right now. As Gracie and I step out of the backroom into Haymakers I can see all of my family and friends gathered around for my big day. I feel like my life is finally complete. I have everything I have ever wanted. Everything I ever hoped for is now at my feet. It's the beginning of the life I always wanted with Jake.

I'm happy to see both my parents smiling as they wait to walk me down the small aisle we've made for the bridal procession.

I have to admit that my parents weren't exactly thrilled when I first told them about my engagement to Jake. It pretty much meant finally putting an end to the dreams they had of me going to college. They felt a tiny bit better about the idea when I mentioned that I'd be co-managing Haymakers. They know it's one of the most successful businesses in Old Town and has been for generations. And I think it also eased their minds a bit that I wouldn't be living in the house alone while they travel around Europe.

Before I head toward the stage where Jake is standing with his brothers Gracie walks down the aisle ahead of me. She joins Riley and Katie Lawrence Wilde, who are already waiting next to the stage. The girls are all in matching, short, pink bridesmaid gowns and pink cowgirl boots.

This is only the second time since graduation that I can remember seeing Jake in anything but jeans and his well-worn cowboy boots. He looks absolutely stunning in his black shadow-stripe tuxedo, matching vest and silver tie—all of the Wilde brothers look amazing.

As soon as Jake lays eyes on me his entire face lights up. My stomach is filled with those pesky butterflies again, but I do my best to breathe deeply as I make my way toward the rest of the bridal party.

Jake's old football coach, Mr. Stanley, also happens to be a minister, so he's agreed to officiate the ceremony for us.

I have to laugh when Coach Stanley says, "I knew the day would eventually come when Jake Wilde would finally grow up and settle down. I just didn't think it would take him ten years to do it."

Jake and I look into each other's eyes as Coach Stanley reads the wedding vows that we both wrote for the occasion. Part of me still wants to pinch myself to make sure I'm not dreaming.

But when Coach Stanley announces that we're husband and wife, and Jake kisses me, I know my dream is now a reality.

I'm Mrs. Harley Wilde. And I'm standing next to Mrs. Riley Wilde, Mrs. Gracie Wilde and Mrs. Katie Lawrence-Wilde. And in just a few minutes we're going to be dancing the night away, while Wilde Riders plays some foot-stomping country music in the bar that I'll be spending the rest of my life running with my husband.

Sneak Peek

See MAX ELLIOT again in…

RYE MUST DIE

An Izzy & Max Paranormal Romantic Comedy
By Dakota Madison & Savannah Young

There's a fine line between sexy alpha and creepy stalker…and Rye has crossed it.

I'm supposed to be dead. Suicide by hanging. But when I regained consciousness I was still alive…still the crazy girl voted "Most Likely to Kill Herself" in high school…still the girl who everyone in Old Town loved to hate.

But one thing had changed. He had saved me. A man wearing all black and riding a motorcycle. He pulled me down from the tree and made sure I was still breathing.

And now he's following me… I just don't know why…But I'm eager to find out.

Prologue

I gasp for breath. Then I cough. The brisk air stings my lungs.

I'm on the cold, hard ground, not hanging from the tree like I'm supposed to be, and I'm definitely not dead.

When I open my eyes I'm glad it's dusk. I don't think I could take the glare of the sun right now. Dusk was always my favorite time of day, when nature's light is fading away.

My neck feels raw, but there's no rope on it. I search around me, but the rope seems to have vanished.

I spot a guy dressed in all black. He's sitting on a black H-D Iron 883, very similar to the motorcycle I ride.

A shiver runs through me when I realize the guy is watching me.

He must have been the one who did it. He cut me down from the tree. I have a vague memory of a struggle. Of strong arms grabbing me and holding me tight. I fought against him, but I was hopelessly outmatched.

I wanted to die but I realized he wasn't going to let me.

Then I blacked out, and woke up on the ground.

I wonder how long he's going to sit there. It's almost like he's guarding me. Then he opens a black satchel on his bike and removes a rope—my rope—and holds it up for me to see.

I feel like he's taunting me with it. Why does this asshole care if I live or die?

When I give him the finger he doesn't respond. He just puts on his dark helmet and speeds away, leaving a cloud of dust in his wake.

I think about some of the other ways I could kill myself, but those methods leave a margin of error that I'm not comfortable with. I don't want to jump in front of a moving truck only to be paralyzed for life and still not dead.

Besides, I'm suddenly hungry and craving a burger and fries in the worst way. I guess today is not the day for me to die.

Six Weeks Later

Another exciting day at the Old Town Antique Shop. I've had only two customers and only one who actually bought something. It's a good thing the building is completely paid for, I live right upstairs, and my grandmother was extremely generous to me in her will. I certainly couldn't afford to run a real business on the pittance the store makes on a weekly basis.

I would have been out of Old Town by now if my grandmother didn't croak. And she didn't stipulate in her will that I had to keep the antique shop running in order to get the money she entrusted to me. I'm the last living member of the Grant family and I now have the honor of running the business that's been in our family for generations.

I glance down at the stash of romance novels I keep hidden under the counter. I know they're cheesy, but right now they're the only things that are keeping me from slashing my wrists when I'm in the bathtub. They give me the slightest bit of hope that maybe someday; someone will love the town pariah. Even the meanest girls in romance novels always get the guy.

I'm deep in a very hot sex scene when I'm startled by the little bell that chimes when the front door opens.

I'm even more surprised by the guy who walks into my shop. Or more like strolls in. He's wearing a wild flowered Hawaiian shirt over a red Green Day T-shirt, faded cargo pants and red converse high tops. He runs his hands through his mop of sun-bleached blond hair, but it doesn't help. Old Town is always windy, but his hair isn't just windblown. It's a little too long and looks shaggy.

He's definitely not from Old Town.

After giving me a quick once over he grins. His grin is too wide and his teeth are too perfect and too white. I already hate him.

"You know we're nowhere near the shore?" I try not to sound as disgusted as this guy is making me.

He laughs. He seems like the kind of guy who laughs easily. I hate him even more.

"I'm not here to surf."

I give him a once over. "You could have fooled me."

He reaches into his jacket pocket and pulls out a shiny business card. He wiggles it in my face so the light overhead reflects off of it.

I rip the card out of his hand just to make the glare stop. "What's wrong with you?"

He laughs again, which makes me even more perturbed. Not that it's difficult to do. Most people are able to get on my bad side pretty quickly.

"Do you want a list?" He raises an eyebrow at me.

I shake my head and examine his card:

Old Town Ghost Tours. Max Elliot, Paranormal Investigator.

Great. Not only is he starting to be the most annoying person on the planet, he's also one of those ghost hunting freaks.

I try to hand the card back to him, but he puts his hands up and shakes them at me. "The card is yours to keep."

If I had a trash can close I'd make a point of throwing the thing inside of it, but the trash can is on the other side of this weirdo and I don't feel like walking past him to get to it.

"You didn't answer my question." I glare at him.

"What's wrong with me?" He looks down at his watch, which I now notice has Mickey Mouse on it. "How much time do you have?"

I give an exasperated sigh. "What can I help you with?"

He grins again. Boy does this guy like to smile a lot. He must think it's charming, and maybe some girls are into that, but I'm definitely not one of them. I can count on one hand the number of times I've smiled so far this year.

And I don't go for blonds and definitely not beach boy blonds with big smiles. I prefer the dark and dangerous type, all in black leather, preferably riding a motorcycle.

"I'd love for you to go out with me, but we can negotiate that later. I'm here to see Alberta Grant. Something tells me that you're not Alberta."

"I'm Izzy Grant," I reply, but I'm not sure why. I don't really want anything to do with this guy.

"What's Izzy short for?"

I frown. "Izzy."

No one calls me by my given name, and definitely not this guy. I only give it out on a need-to-know basis.

"Okay, Izzy. How can I find Alberta?"

I narrow my eyes at him. "You're obviously not from around here."

"Why would you say that?"

"Well, you're not wearing jeans and cowboy boots for starters." *And you have no idea my grandmother is dead.* Everyone in town knows that.

He points to his business card lying on the counter. "Just moved here. I'm trying to start a business."

"In Old Town?"

He nods. "I'm going to capitalize on the popularity of the Tawnee Mountain Resort. The guests need some nighttime entertainment and ghost hunting is really popular right now."

I don't feel like stating the obvious. That there's no such thing as ghosts.

I decide to play with the guy because he's annoying and it's not like I have anything better to do.

"Alberta isn't here right now, but I can take you to her."

He grins again. Oh how I wish I could just slap that big grin right off of his perfect, beach boy face. Then he looks around the place. "Are you sure you aren't too busy?"

I narrow my gaze at him. "I'll make time for you."

"See, you already like me."

If he only knew.

I lock up the store and hang up my OUT TO LUNCH sign. Max follows me to the small parking lot on the side of the store.

I stop in front of my old Harley H-D Iron 883. "Do you want a ride? I've got an extra helmet."

He laughs. "There is no way I'm riding on the back of a chick's motorcycle."

I point a finger in his face. "I'm not a chick. And if you ever call me that again, I'll rip your dick off."

He puts his hands up. "Okay, chill. It's just an expression. Can we take my car instead?"

I glance at the bright red Mini Cooper parked at the other end of the parking lot. "That's not a real vehicle. That's a clown car."

"This isn't just any Mini Cooper. It's a special limited edition."

I frown. "Just an FYI. If you plan on living in Old Town you'll attract a lot less attention if you're driving a pickup, preferably a Ford or a Dodge Ram."

He grins. Another one of those huge grins that irritate every nerve in my body. "Who says I don't want attention?"

I shake my head. "Never mind."

I'm short, only about five feet two inches, and I'm worried about fitting inside that car. I have no idea how Max, who's easily a foot taller than me, fits inside of it.

"Okay, we can take your car," I agree, but only because I want to see how he squeezes inside that thing.

He pulls his keys from his pocket and starts throwing them in the air like he's juggling with them. The guy has no shortage of ways to completely annoy me.

To my surprise Max fits into his car better than I imaged he would. He's got the seat pushed back as far as it will go, so his legs aren't cramped.

"You could buy a bigger car," I say as I snap on my seat belt. "Being such a big guy."

He laughs. "Are you kidding? This car is a chick magnet. I've known you less than fifteen minutes and I've already got you inside of it."

When he winks at me I feel a little bile rise in my throat like I want to vomit. "Just so we're clear. You're not my type."

He waves the comment off like a mosquito. "I'm everyone's type."

"Not mine," I repeat.

"You won't know for sure until you've had a chance to test the goods." Then he winks at me.

Now I'm really going to be sick. "I'm not interested in testing any of your goods. Do you want to see my grandmother or not?"

He heaves a sigh. "Tell me where to drive."

Five minutes later we pull up to the Old Town Cemetery. As soon as Max parks the car he turns and looks at me. "Is this your idea of a joke?"

"You're the ghost hunter. Isn't this like your Valhalla or something?"

He rolls his eyes at me. "Most graveyards aren't haunted. Spirits like to stay close to loved ones, or places they were most familiar with before they died."

"Whatever you say." I open the door and hop out of his clown car.

I'm surprised when he follows. Part of me thought he'd just turn the engine back on and speed away.

As I open the cemetery gate I'm overwhelmed with sadness...again. It's been happening a lot lately...ever since my grandmother died. She was the last of my relatives, and now I'm alone in the world. Not that I'm not used to being a loner. I'm known for it. But being alone, without any family to anchor me, makes me feel truly lost.

Alberta Grant wasn't the nicest person in the world, but she was my rock. She lived to be ninety, and from what I've heard around town, spent at least forty of those years being a cantankerous old broad, who was both feared and admired.

I seem to be following in her footsteps. Except for the admired part. People in Old Town say I'm freak and a bitch and tend to steer clear.

And I'm okay with that.

When I find my grandmother's headstone I clear away the leaves that have fallen on it.

"How did she die?" Max asks. His tone is actually sincere. He's finally dropped the overdone surfer-boy salesman act.

"She was old. Ninety."

He nods. "Do you miss her?"

"More than I ever thought I would."

He's actually quiet as he stands there with me. He's slightly attractive when he's not talking. It's when he opens his pie hole that he's a complete turn off.

As we drive back toward the antique shop I have a brief moment of panic when Max passes right by it.

"You missed my stop."

"I know," he says matter-of-factly.

"Let me out. Now." I can feel my pulse start to race. I briefly consider jumping out of the car, but I'm not wearing my leather today so the pavement would definitely hurt as I slid across it.

"It's okay." When Max glances over at me, I can see concern in his eyes. "I'm just going to take you to lunch. My treat."

I take in a deep breath and try to calm my frayed nerves. "Lunch?"

"You put an OUT TO LUNCH sign on your door," he reminds me. "So I'm taking you to lunch."

"You'll do anything for a date, won't you?"

"So you're actually going on a date with me?" He grins. "And here I thought you were a tough girl."

I huff. "Do I have a choice? You kind of have me trapped in your clown car."

When he glances over at me his eyes have turned serious. "You always have a choice. Don't ever forget that."

I nod, but we're both quiet as we head back into the center of Old Town.

If only all guys thought the way he does, my life wouldn't be a complete and total mess.

OLD TOWN COUNTRY ROMANCE series:

COMING SOON
THE TAWNEE MOUNTAIN series
By Savannah Young & Sierra Avalon

ANOTHER MAZZY MONDAY (Book One)
JUST A SUZIE SUNDAY (Book Two)

About the Author

Savannah Young grew up in rural northwest New Jersey in a place very similar to the fictional Old Town, which is featured in her books. When she's not at her computer creating spicy stories, Savannah is traveling to exotic locales or spending time with her husband and their bloodhounds.

Follow Savannah on Facebook:
https://www.facebook.com/KarenMuellerBrysonAuthor
Savannah's Blog: http://karenmuellerbryson.tumblr.com

CPSIA information can be obtained at www.ICGtesting.com
Printed in the USA
LVOW01s1809250615

443875LV00014B/575/P